Eileen Barwick was born in the East End of London, in the early 50s, where she grew up until her Mid-Teens. She is married and has two sons. She went to live in New Zealand for couple of years. Following her return she qualified as a nurse and remained in the profession until her retirement. Eileen moved to southern Ireland with the second husband and soon found a desire to learn new skills. Following a Diploma course in creative writing, she embarked on writing her first ever novel: *The Golden Threads*.

Firstly and most importantly, I thank my husband, John. Through his patience, tolerance and ever listening ear, I was persuaded to write my first novel. John also gave me encouragement to believe in myself, my abilities and to attempt to have my work published.

Secondly, I have to thank the characters of my early years growing up in London. Many have now passed on, but their wit, humour and way of life, has given me a rich resource to work with.

Eileen Barwick

The Golden Threads

AUSTIN MACAULEY PUBLISHERS™
LONDON • CAMBRIDGE • NEW YORK • SHARJAH

Copyright © Eileen Barwick 2022

The right of Eileen Barwick to be identified as author of this work has been asserted by the author in accordance with sections 77 and 78 of the Copyright, Designs and Patents Act 1988.

All rights reserved. No part of this publication may be reproduced, stored in a retrieval system, or transmitted in any form or by any means, electronic, mechanical, photocopying, recording, or otherwise, without the prior permission of the publishers.

Any person who commits any unauthorised act in relation to this publication may be liable to criminal prosecution and civil claims for damages.

This is a work of fiction. Names, characters, businesses, places, events, locales, and incidents are either the products of the author's imagination or used in a fictitious manner. Any resemblance to actual persons, living or dead, or actual events is purely coincidental.

A CIP catalogue record for this title is available from the British Library.

ISBN 9781398464322 (Paperback)
ISBN 9781398464339 (Hardback)
ISBN 9781398464353 (ePub e-book)
ISBN 9781398464346 (Audiobook)

www.austinmacauley.com

First Published 2022
Austin Macauley Publishers Ltd®
1 Canada Square
Canary Wharf
London
E14 5AA

Synopsis for the Novel
The Golden Threads

Nellie was brought up by her grandparents living in the East End of London.

At the age of 19 years, she was able to work as a 'Nippy' in a large J Lyons and Co Corner House in London where she was to meet her lifelong friend Connie. Nellie soon found the love of her life and married Tommy Brown, but her idyllic life was soon to change with the outbreak of WW2. The comfortable safe routine of her life would be completely turned on its head.

Nellie decided to help where she could in the war effort, so she joined the Women's Land Army and was posted to a farm in Norfolk, only to return to London after a couple of years following yet another tragedy.

Nellie was to meet many characters during wartime as after the Land Army, she then became an ambulance driver and going into recently bombed areas of London, even fearlessly going in during the raids.

Rebuilding her life post-wartime with its mix of devastation, sadness and a good sprinkling of humour thrown in for good measure, would Nellie Brown find happiness and love again?

Chapter 1

"Bugger off, you little sods, I will be along to speak to your mothers," said Nellie Brown.

"Leave off, old lady, you can't catch us. Anyway, you don't know where we live," shouted back one of the young boys.

"I know where you live, Kenny Smith, and I know that you are the main culprit."

It suddenly went quiet outside.

"It takes me 10 bloody minutes to get myself up out of my chair now and get to the front door only to find no bugger there," she grumbled as she shuffled her way to the kitchen. "I might as well make myself a cup of tea now I am up."

Just then, she heard the letter box open and a small voice called out, "Sorry, Gran, we were only having a bit of fun. We won't do it again, promise."

Nellie smiled to herself as she began to pour the boiling water into the small teapot, which was then placed onto a tray next to a bone china cup and saucer. 'Knock down ginger' the game was called in the East End of London; kids would think it funny to knock on people's doors then run and hide.

Nellie made her way back into the sitting room, placed the tea tray on the small table in front of her then settled back into her favourite chair, which was now getting a bit worn and threadbare in places, but to Nellie it was comfortable and comforting, like having a pair of long arms wrapped around her. Nellie, as she sipped on her tea, began to reflect back to her own youth and how so very different it was from today.

Was our generation so carefree and mischievous, I think not. From a young age, boys had to help their fathers and the girls their mothers with the daily chores; often, the families were bigger and generally the older children looked after the younger siblings. Financially for many, money was scarce and hardships plenty full.

"Stop grumbling, Nellie," she told herself. "Each generation is different, there is always good times as well as bad and thankfully, the young people today do not know what their future may hold just as we didn't, thank god.

"I do reflect though on how those years have flown by and the friends we made along the way, most have gone now."

Nellie sipped her last mouthful of tea and sat back in her chair. "I think I might just close my eyes for a few minutes while I wait."

The sound of the clock ticking its gentle rhythm just as it had since the first day she had received it, was like an old friend just whispering in her ear and soothing her off to sleep.

Nellie from the day she moved into her Victorian house had kept it as clean as a new pin, it had a lovely smell of polish (which was not surprising at it was cleaned daily). Nellie may have been in her 80s but her standards never wavered; it maintained a calm and relaxed feeling, so it was not surprising that sleep came over her quickly.

"You look really bonnie, lass, we are so proud of you, Nellie," said her grandparents as she stood before them in her uniform.

Nellie had been brought up by her grandparents as her mother had died in childbirth whilst having her and by all accounts her father had run off with another woman before Nellie was born and was never seen again, so there was never any mention of him. If there were, it was met with a stern look and the conversation was swiftly changed; so strong after all the years was the bitterness and anger still. The dark look that would cross her grandfather's face, Nellie felt that he would have murdered him had he shown his face even after this length of time.

Her grandmother had been born in Edinburgh and had come down to work in London when she was a young woman, where she had met Nellie's grandfather and apparently it was love at first sight. He was a dock worker and it was pure chance that they met, but they soon became inseparable.

Nellie's grandparents were the absolute love of her life; she knew as she grew up that they had given her the best that they could afford. Her grandmother taught her how to cook, make jams and cakes, sew, crochet and knit. Everything she had been taught was done with love and fun, even teaching her how to manage the household finances and budgeting. Really, Nellie had been taught all the tools for a successful independent future.

Her grandfather would take her out for long walks after Sunday dinner, leaving her grandmother to clean up and then sit and have five minutes' 'peace and quiet' as she called it, which Nellie knew to mean a snooze.

During the walks, her grandfather would teach her about any birds or insects that they might see, anything that would expand Nellie's knowledge of the world around her and beyond. During autumn and winter, they would go foraging along the river bank, often picking blackberries along the way.

"Hey lass, nothing beats a blackberry and apple pie with custard, especially the ones your gran makes."

Nellie had been taught by her grandmother how to make jams and chutneys, so during winter-time, very little was wasted and the larder was always well stocked with home-made produce. Often walking many miles and being out for at least a couple of hours, Nellie loved spending quality time with her granddad. In time to come, they would be very precious memories to revisit in her mind. He, like her grandmother, taught her so much, mostly how to appreciate the world around her. When they would return home, the routine was that her granddad sat in the front room with a cup of tea, (which never took long to make as the kettle was always on the stove, simmering) while Nellie helped her gran in the kitchen getting their tea ready, which they were more than ready for. The routine was consistent and comforting.

Life for Nellie in the east of London was as idyllic as if she was a princess in a palace, the main ingredient being love in bucket-loads.

The bond between the three of them was very strong, each being the main focus of their lives. On occasions in the evening, they would just sit and talk about various topics and sometimes they spoke about Nellie's mother, making comparison on personality traits, looks and interests. The memory box which contained all the precious things they had saved of their daughter's life had a single photo inside with other small items of huge sentimental value. Nellie would often feel that such a small box with just a few things inside could hold such a strong mix of sadness and love, and her grandparents treasured the box as if it contained a million pounds, but she loved to see the photo of a mother she never knew.

Nellie was now a young woman of 19 years, but legally still under her grandfather's control, as in the year of 1936 a young woman under the age of 21 years was not allowed to do anything without parental consent. In Nellie's case, in the absence of a father, it was her grandfather's role.

It was going to take some persuading to convince her grandmother and grandfather that it would be a good move working at a Lyons Corner House.

"You realise that it will be very hard work and you will be on your feet all day?" said her grandmother. "It will also be a long day as you will need to leave here early and be home late. What about eating regularly, we don't want you fading away to nothing, girl."

Nellie's grandmother was an absolute treasure to Nellie, but sometimes, as she was getting older, she felt that she needed to be a bit more independent. Her grandparents had brought her up very well, not too strict, but enough that she knew right from wrong and would never do anything to shame or embarrass them, but she really wanted this job and tried hard to get them to understand that it was all very respectable and that it was a good company with a good name. Nellie came up with an idea that might help to sway them into allowing her this chance.

"How about on Saturday, I treat you both to afternoon tea at one of the tea houses so that you can see for yourselves what it is like?"

"I don't know if I care to go into London on one of those trains," said her granny.

"Come on, Nan, it will be an adventure."

Eventually, all the persuading had the desired effect and Nellie was going to be a Nippy. (This was the title that the girls working for the company were given.)

There in the parlour of her grandparent's house, Nellie proudly stood with her hair all pinned up neatly, ready to set off to her first day of training. She asked her granny to check that there were no stray strands of hair trying to escape and that she looked clean and tidy. This was as much as anything to allow her grandmother to still feel important and involved, although to Nellie, this was to be the start of a new, independent life. Nellie possessed a slim figure, was of medium height with long wavy dark brown hair, she had her mother's blue eyes that held a cheeky sparkle, bow-shaped lips and peaches and cream complexion. Now with her hair curled up on top of her head and the merest hint of makeup, it brought a lump to the throats of her grandparents as they realised that she was now a grown woman, which made them proud but anxious as they realised that she would catch the eye of many men.

Nellie got the train from her nearest station and headed off into London to Orchard House where she had attended her initial interview but this time, is was to begin her training as a Nippy.

She sat next to a girl of about the same age as herself; 18 years was the minimum age to be a Nippy. They introduced themselves and exchanged other polite information during the journey.

Connie Doyle was originally from Galway and had a lovely soft Irish accent (which Nellie at times struggled to understand). She had thick auburn hair, which she also had pinned up, green eyes and pale but clear skin with an air of gentle friendliness about her. The girls chatted away as they travelled into London, exchanging their backgrounds and interests.

Connie explained that she had moved over from Ireland, leaving her family behind.

There was not much in the way of employment or opportunities where she had moved from, which was only a small village, so she persuaded her parents to allow her to move to England. She was originally supposed to be staying with an elderly aunt who lived in Wales, but she felt that it would not be so different from where she had moved from. So here she was in London, starting out on a new path the same as Nellie. She explained that she was just living in a one-room accommodation which was not ideal, but once she was working full-time, then things would hopefully change.

The girls who by now were very comfortable in each other's company made their way to the building where they hoped their new life in the adult world would prove both exciting and rewarding.

The lecture started with a stern-faced woman who looked like she would not suffer any nonsense. "Good morning, girls."

"Good morning, Miss Bird," the girls replied in unison.

"Today, we shall explain to you the standard that we expect of our Nippy waitresses, both whilst you are on duty and when you are not. This afternoon, we will then be setting tables. I am sure that you already think you know how to do this, but I can assure you that it quite possibly is not to Lyons Tea house' standard."

"Crikey, she is not one to mess with," both the girls said almost in unison during their tea break.

"Perhaps as we all get to know the rules and one another, she probably will soften," said Nellie hopefully.

Returning home after her first day of training, Nellie had to admit to feeling both mentally and physically exhausted.

"There is just so much to learn, but having said that, I know that I am going to love working there. Everyone is just so friendly and helpful." Nellie flopped into an armchair, still wearing her coat.

"Right then, my girl, go and get changed. There will be a hot cup of tea for you when you come down and dinner is almost ready to serve. Once we have eaten, we can sit and you can tell us all about your day."

After dinner and everything was tidy again, they all sat on the comfy chairs to hear how the first day went. Nellie really struggled to keep her eyes open, but was also full of excitement as she shared her day's events.

"There seems so much to learn, I thought setting a table was just about putting cutlery and glasses on the table. We also were instructed on how we were expected to behave when on duty, I am sure that in time it would all be second nature to us all.

"I have made a friend already today; she is from Galway in Ireland but has lived here for a while now with relatives. She is really attractive so I bet when we start serving real customers, she will get plenty of tips. She has the most gorgeous hair colouring, red with golden threads through it, and lovely pale clear skin, but it is her voice that will win the customers over. It sounds like gentle music, so soft and lilting. Connie also has a lovely gentle nature about her too, I am sure that we will become firm friends.

"We also learned today that the company has a sports centre and social club that the employees have full use of. Apparently, dances are frequently held there and dance competitions; it all looks very exciting."

"You just concentrate on learning to do your job properly and not worry too much about going to parties, there will be plenty of time for that when you are older, my girl," said her grandfather.

"Granddad, I don't think that I will have the energy to party. I think that after a day's work, I will be too tired for anything other than tea and bed," replied Nellie.

Nellie woke with her gran standing over her holding a mug of hot chocolate, she must have drifted off.

"I think it is time for you to go to bed and get a good night's sleep, you will need your energy for another day tomorrow. Sleep well, my love, we are glad that you had a good day and have made a friend. It will get easier as you settle into a routine."

Although it was much earlier than she would normally retire for the night, she had to admit that she was eager to get her head on her pillow.

"Good night to you both," she said as she gave each grandparent a kiss.

As soon as Nellie's head hit the pillow, she was gone.

"I hope that the lass takes her time and settles before she starts getting involved with parties and lads," whispered her grandfather as the elderly couple retired to their own bedroom. He was realising now that Nellie was no longer a child but a young woman and becoming independent.

"She will, George, she will," smiled his wife.

Gradually, Nellie settled into a routine and found herself feeling less tired or stressed as everything was becoming more familiar. Getting up early was easier and her breakfast was there ready on the table as her grandparents were always up before her.

"I am just so lucky to have you both looking after me so well, what would I do without you!"

Fortunately, it was just as well no one knew what was waiting around the corner to change their futures forever.

The few weeks of training were over and now Nellie as a fully trained Nippy had to get out and start to serve real customers. She would mentally go through the checklist of how to wear her uniform correctly, ensuring that; the black dress was the correct length, her hat that sat on her pinned up hair was clean and pressed with the monogram in the centre. Buttons, and there were numerous, were sewn in with red cotton, shoes were well-polished and her plain black stockings were ladder and snag-free, the white collar and cuffs of her uniform along with the apron were well-laundered.

Nellie smiled to herself as she went out from the changing room, confident that everything was as it should be before facing their superior who was waiting to inspect them and ensure that they were fit to step out to the public.

As expected, it had been a busy day, although the time had seem to fly by, the tea rooms never at any time appeared empty, such was its popularity. People would be there in the morning for tea or coffee, lunchtime was always a very busy time of day, then in the afternoon, high tea would be served; more often it would be mainly women of leisure.

All of the girls smiled throughout the day and remained cheerful; after all, no one wants to be served by someone miserable. Their superior often appeared presumably to ensure that everything was as it should be and would walk around ensuring that the customers were happy.

Nellie settled in well and became a valued member of staff, always willing to help out and change her days off at short notice if required. She managed well and was now not so exhausted at the end of the day, continuing to enjoy her work and glad that the decision to become a Nippy had been the right one. Nellie and Connie had become close friends and together began to enjoy some of the sports activities and began to frequent the social activities. Although alcohol was served at these events, both girls were under no illusion that everyone kept a close eye on them. Even though they were off-duty, their behaviour was expected to always be exemplary; also, a good few of the employees were under the drinking age so soft drinks only were consumed.

One day when they arrived at work, there were a couple of new girls just out of training and they looked anxious and nervous. Nellie remembered that feeling very well.

"It's good fun when you have been here a while. It is a bit nerve-racking to start, but you will soon get used to it. My name is Nellie by the way and this is Connie."

"Hi, I'm Grace," replied one of the new girls.

"Well, have a good day and we may see you later," encouraged Nellie.

Sure enough, at the end of another very busy day, the girls met up again whilst changing out of their uniforms back into civvies.

"How did it go, girls?" enquired Nellie.

"Pretty well, although there is one tutor who scared us half to death with her stern mannerisms."

Both Nellie and Connie looked at one another and smiled.

"We know who you are referring to, but trust us, so long as you do as she tells you to, you will find that she does soften after a while and is actually a really nice person, once she is happy that you understand the rules and follow them."

Over the months, Grace, Nellie and Connie became close friends and enjoyed working and socialising together.

"I was wondering, us three get on so well but we all live a distance from each other and work, what do you think about us getting somewhere closer to work to live? We can share the bills?" asked Connie, who was now 21 and the eldest of the three.

"I do not think that I should have too much problem," replied Grace, "as I live with my older brother and his family. My parents live up North and I wanted to work down here in London so I should think that my brother would be glad of the space again."

"So what about you, Nellie?" asked Connie.

"I am not sure how my grandparents will take it, they are very protective of me. It was hard enough convincing them to let me work at the tea house. You may need to give me a bit of time to persuade them."

"There is no rush, but it might work out better for us in the long run; we will not be so tired as we will have less travelling time," said Connie.

So Nellie was left to decide when the time might be right to approach the subject at home.

Over the next few weeks, Nellie gently and gradually introduced the subject then one day, her grandmother said, "For goodness' sake, girl, you have been skirting around the subject of moving out, so just come right out with it."

Nellie went on to explain the reasons for moving nearer into London and the plans that the girls had made.

"Well, I can see that the idea makes sense, but you are all such young, vulnerable women, we must talk to your grandfather and it is for him to make the final decision," replied her grandmother.

So later that evening, with much persuading and using her feminine wiles, it was agreed that provisionally she could make enquiries about suitable accommodation, but with a condition that before an agreement was made, her grandmother would check the suitability of the area and the landlady of the property.

"Apparently, the company can help its employees to find accommodation," said Connie.

"No need," replied Grace. "When I was telling my brother of our plans, he told me he knows of a property where some tenants have just left and by all accounts the land lady is excellent."

So enquiries and arrangements were made, then the three girls headed off to Bethnal Green in London to take a look at the place.

"It is just what we were looking for," said the girls in unison.

"If you do not mind before I can agree, would it be possible for my grandmother to come and see you?" Nellie asked, feeling a little embarrassed by making this request.

"Absolutely, I agree totally that she should want to come and see for herself where you are planning on residing," agreed the prospective landlady.

"Nan, this is Mrs Jennings and Mrs Jennings, this is my grandmother."

"Oh please call me Agnes," said Nellie's gran.

"Very pleased to meet you. I am Mary."

Tea was offered, biscuits and cakes consumed, conversation flowed easily.

"Right then," said Mary, "let's have the guided tour, mind you it won't take too long." She laughed.

The property was very clean and tidy, there was a small sitting room allocated where the girls could sit in privacy, and then the other rooms downstairs were Mrs Jennings' private areas. Upstairs, there were two bedrooms of a comfortable size, each had a single bed with beautiful floral bedspreads covering them, there was a small wardrobe and dressing table which appeared to be highly polished and well-maintained and there were even flowers in a vase in each room. From the bedrooms across the landing, there was also a bathroom, again not a large area but contained a small slipper type bath which in these times was a luxury indeed, a sink and flushing lavatory.

"My word," said Nellie's granny, "you girls have certainly picked a little palace here, I wouldn't mind moving in myself, there's no going out in the cold night air with a candle for the outside lavatory." Many homes in London at that time only had the outside toilets.

Nellie felt immensely happy, as it appeared that the house was certainly meeting her nan's approval. They continued up another small flight of stairs, where there was another bedroom, slightly smaller in size than the others but with the same furniture and to the fresh clean standard as the others. From here, they returned to the sitting room for another cup of tea.

"Right then, girls, before we come to any agreements, you need to know the rules of the house. There are to be no gentlemen friends in the house after 10 pm and they are only allowed in this sitting room. The front door will be locked at 11 pm unless there is a special occasion or circumstance which I would need to be informed of so as I do not lock you out. As you can see, I have standards regarding cleanliness and I expect them to be maintained. Rent is to be paid on time without exception, I will prepare and cook the meals for you and if you so choose, I will do the washing but you can do your own ironing. If all of these conditions are acceptable, I am happy to allow you girls to live here and I feel sure that we will get on and have a grand old time."

Nellie looked to her friends and her nan and all had smiles on their faces, so arrangements for moving in were made and they asked if they could go back up and choose their rooms in readiness. The two older women sat and had a good old chat, they got on very well together and by the time that they all left, friendships had been formed.

"Well, I must admit that the property, and most certainly the landlady, are all excellent. I do not have the worries and concerns that I had initially and I am confident that you will all be well-looked-after and that Mrs Jennings will keep a sharp eye on you all."

Nellie now was filled with a mixture of happiness which was tinged with a little sadness. She could see in her grandparents' eyes that they were pleased and proud of her but letting her go into the outside world and fly as all birds must do was hard for them.

"I will visit as often as I can and you know where I am so please do come and see me."

The day of departure arrived and Nellie with her possessions in a suitcase waved her beloved grandparents goodbye as the tears flowed down her cheeks. Just as well that Nellie could not see that both her grandparents were also shedding tears as the love and joy of their lives was now grown up and making her own way in the world.

Chapter 2

The three girls settled into their new home with lots of giggling excitement. Nellie and Connie had the two bedrooms on the first floor and young Grace, who was the youngest, quietest and the shyest, had the top room. Once they had put their few belongings in the rooms and makeup on their dressing tables, they then went downstairs to have a cup of tea with Mrs Jennings. Initially, the girls did not know much about the private life of their landlady, but gradually as friendships grew and so did the confidence in one another, stories were shared by one and all. It appeared that Mrs Jennings had lost her husband in the First World War and they never had the chance to start a family. Afraid of how she was going to make ends meet, Mary, as they now were allowed to call their landlady, decided because the house was too large for one she would open it up for paying tenants and so be able to makes ends meet with a few little extra for treats, and it also gave her some company.

As time progressed, there forged a very strong bond between all of the females and Mary became more like a mother figure.

Working in the Lyons Corner House tea shop in Piccadilly was like heaven to the girls. The store was five-storeys high, most of the stores had four or five levels, with hairdressing salons, a food hall where many speciality products from the Corner House kitchens could be brought. Each floor had its own restaurant style, and they all had orchestras playing to the diners almost continuously throughout the day and evening. There were also telephone booths; although very few people possessed phones in their private homes, it was still mainly for business unless you were very rich. On the social side of things, they had a club where dances were held. But as the girls knew, they were expected to work hard; it was a 54-hour week.

The girls loved it all, meeting people from different walks of life, some more pleasant than others, and getting the attention of men whether wanted or not was quite common, but they were expected to be equally as pleasant to them all. Lyons claimed that the marriage rate for a Nippy was higher than any other class of working girl and that the job was of course excellent training for becoming a future housewife.

"Well, I am not looking to settle down with any man at the moment. I am having too much of a good time, also Lyons do not employ married ladies, so I am not ready to give this up just yet, are you?" asked Nellie.

"Not bloody likely," replied Connie; a comment that was echoed by Grace.

"Really, Connie, if only your parents back in Ireland could hear your language now and don't let Mrs Jennings catch you swearing."

"She might give you your marching orders," replied Grace.

"I know, I knew so few bad words until I moved to London, still I will watch my tongue in future. Mind you, there are a few men that come in to the restaurant that I would like to tell to bugger off," replied Connie.

The girls all laughed and agreed with this sentiment.

Life ticked along nicely and the girls and Mary Jennings formed a very strong bond, in a way Mary felt like these girls could be her daughters and she had become very fond of them. Each girl had her own character; there was Nellie, who was very polite, well-behaved and always well-turned-out, but she could flare if there was something she felt strongly about and did not suffer fools gladly, but equally she was very loyal to her family and friends. Connie was a delight to listen to, with her soft Irish lilt, she had the voice that could send babies off to sleep with a lullaby. But you would be a fool to cross her, as she too would tell you straight if the need arose. Grace was the quietest. She could be rather shy until she felt comfortable either with a person or a situation, but being the youngest of the three, both Nellie and Connie protected her as though she were the younger sibling. So all in all the relationships worked, mind you now and then there could be the odd spat.

"Who has nicked my pink jumper?" shouted Nellie one morning.

"Why would anyone take anything of yours?" replied Connie.

"Well, it was there yesterday in my wardrobe and now it's gone."

"Could you have left it somewhere and just forgotten?"

"I am 20 years old, not 90, I have not yet lost me bloody marbles."

"What is all the shouting about, I can hear you downstairs," asked Mary.

"It's Nellie here, she thinks someone has pinched her pink jumper and is throwing accusations around," grumbled Connie.

Mary looked at Nellie. "I am sorry, I took it down and washed it, I saw you wear it the other day and thought I would freshen it up for you, sorry."

"So, do we get an apology?" asked Connie, as she stood with her arms crossed over her chest.

"OK, I suppose I did jump to conclusions."

"Is that it, your apology?"

"Sorry," said Nellie, slightly shamefaced.

Whilst Nellie was working the next day, which again was busy, Nellie had the uncanny feeling that she was being watched, but in a busy crowded restaurant that could have been anyone, or no one, but it was just that sixth sense feeling that you sometimes get.

The day as usual started with all the girls attending the staff canteen where they were given instructions for the day. Nellie and the others went about their duties with speed and efficiency as was expected of them as a Nippy. With now some experience, Nellie loved it there, she loved the *buzz* of the constant chatter and laughter of the customer, as well as the background music of the orchestra. This was the work she had dreamed of and now she was living it. As hard as it was, the rewards were good with an added bonus of being often well-tipped by the customers; at the end of the day, it would amount to a fair bit of extra money. Today, though, for no obvious reason, she could not shake off the feeling that she was being watched, but eventually she had to dismiss this as just imagination. Also, having another busy day, she soon forgot such fanciful notions.

That evening, Nellie asked, "Fancy us three going to the local pub for a drink tonight just for a change?"

"I was going to sit and listen to the radio and read," replied Connie.

"I don't mind going out," said Grace.

"Come on, Connie, you can read later when we return, I don't suppose we shall be that late. Anyway, we are only young once, don't be such an old woman."

"Bloody cheeky, mate," said Connie, "I will show you how to have a good time."

With that, the girls went off to their rooms to smarten up before heading off to the local.

"Won't be too late, Mary, just going down the road," shouted out Connie to Mary who was in her own sitting room.

"Just you girls mind how you go, behave yourselves and don't speak to any strangers."

"What's the fun in that?" laughed Nellie as all three left the house and headed off down the road.

"What the heck do we drink?" asked the young naive Grace.

"I have heard some girls at the social club at work ask for a gin and orange, shall we give that a try?" replied Connie.

So three gin and orange drinks were ordered. By the time they were on their fourth and were giggling over silly things that had occurred in work, they decided that they should be heading off home. Now after each consuming four drinks, and with the girls never having any experience of alcohol, they headed out into the night air, where the effects really took a hold.

"Nellie!" cried Grace. "I think I'm going to be sick."

When the girls entered the house, they thought that they were quiet, but no such luck. Mary appeared as they attempted to navigate the stairs.

"Well, looks like you three have had a good time." This comment had a definite tone to it and it was not a happy one. "Well, if any of you are sick or make a mess, then it will be you that cleans it up. Goodnight."

"Who put that drum in my head?"

"I don't know but they have put the whole bleeding band in mine," moaned the girls the next day.

"Morning, girls," said Mary with a beam on her face. "Fried breakfast is served."

Lesson learned, laughed Mary, *they won't be repeating that too often.*

"The time Nellie had been living with Mary and the girls passed quickly ," said Nellie.

During this time, Nellie had frequently returned to see her grandparents and she would regale them of all that had gone on, how many famous faces she had seen and tried to draw pictures in their minds of the shops at Christmas with their bright lights, window displays and the decorations in the streets.

"Oh you should see the window displays in the likes of John Lewis, Liberties and many other stores, it is truly magical."

Trying hard to encourage them to go into London one evening with her to see the delights for themselves, but her grandparents would just reply, "We are too old to be bothered, dear, all those crowds pushing and shoving, no, we just enjoy you telling us all about it in the comfort of our own home."

Nellie realised with a saddened heart that they were growing old and the enthusiasm of youth was no longer there. She did not notice it whilst living with them and seeing them daily, but now when she visited, it was more obvious and she told herself that she should make a special effort to visit more often as they so enjoyed her visits and spoiled her rotten when she was there.

"Let's go out on the town tonight and celebrate the fact that we have lived and worked together for two years and not killed one another. There is a dance on at the local hall," suggested Nellie.

That evening, while Nellie got herself ready, she looked in the mirror as she applied her make up. "You're not such a bad looker, miss, once you have done yourself up a bit." Nellie had thick dark hair which hung in waves and framed her heart-shaped face beautifully, she was also blessed with good skin that caught the sun and gave her a healthy glow, with long eyelashes and those full bow-shaped lips she stood out in the crowd. Putting on her red dress and beige shoes, she somehow felt different tonight and was looking forward to going out with the girls.

Entering the hall, the three friends found themselves some seats and sat listening to the local band playing. Since their last experience of drinking, they decided to stick to soft drinks only; they did not want a repeat performance, plus they wanted to enjoy the evening and relax. There were a few local faces that they recognised and some that also worked with them at Lyons. Connie was the first to be asked up for a dance and she did look gorgeous. With her red hair swept up in a bun, and wearing an emerald green dress that brought out the colour of her eyes and when she spoke, the men must have thought that they had died and gone to heaven, having such a soft gentle voice with its Irish lilt. Grace was next invited to dance with a good-looking young man. She appeared very timid, but when she sat back down again, she said that she had enjoyed herself and that he would return for another dance later on.

"Hello, gorgeous, can I buy you a drink?"

As Nellie turned, she realised it was to her he was speaking. Here was a very handsome young man with a cheeky smile and a glint in his eye and for no reason that could be explained, Nellie in that moment felt that this was the man she would one day marry.

Chapter 3

"I have seen you working in the Lyons tea house in Piccadilly," said Tommy, "but I have never been close enough to actually speak to you."

"So I did not imagine all those times when I felt that someone was watching me," replied Nellie. "How did you know that I would be at this dance, have you been following me?"

"No, not following you as such, but after the first time I saw you, I wanted to get to know you and ask you out before some other guy did, so I made enquiries as to where you lived and took a chance that you would be here tonight for the dance."

"I am not sure that I like the idea of you following me, it's unsettling."

"Sorry, I have never meant to upset you, but you are so beautiful, you stood out from all the other girls to me and I did not want to risk never getting to know you."

Nellie, although slightly uneasy, decided that he seemed a nice, good-looking, confident young man who had a cheeky smile about him, so she allowed herself to take a chance on him.

The relationship flourished and they became very close. Her friends all thought that he was a 'good catch' so Nellie eventually after months of courtship invited him to join her on one of her visits to her grandparents' house.

"He seems to be a nice young man," said her grandmother whilst she and Nellie made the sandwiches for tea.

"Yes, I must say that I have grown rather fond of him and he treats me so well," replied Nellie. "What do you think Granddad thinks of him? He does seem to be asking Tommy lots of questions like where does he live, what job does he do, are his parents alive."

"Don't mind your granddad, he loves you so much. Just remember he is looking after you and your future and is making sure that Tommy is a suitable man for you."

"Nan!" exclaimed Nellie. "We are not talking wedding bells just yet."

"I see the way that you look at each other so we are just making sure," replied her grandmother. The two women laughed as they took the sandwiches into the parlour.

One evening, Tommy and Nellie went to one of the local pubs where one chap was playing the piano, so they joined in the singing, along with other drinkers. Connie and her young gentleman, Pete, also came along and joined in. Connie had met Pete whilst at work. He had started to chat her up and after three or four attempts of Pete asking her out, Connie finally agreed. The girls still continued to live with Mary in her house. Young Grace had made friends with some others where they worked and often went out with them. Remembering the bad night of drinking, she stayed well clear of alcohol, so she was never a worry to Mary on that score.

Courtships for both girls was progressing well and many a happy time was spent walking along the embankment in London or in Regents Park, where they would often take a picnic with them and spend a complete day there. Nellie was so happy and life seemed just bliss, with a good job, where she was content and the now love of her life at her side, things had never been better.

"Why have I not yet met your parents?" asked Nellie one day.

Tommy informed her that his father worked for the government and that they lived abroad and he did not really see much of them.

"That's a shame."

"Actually, it suits me fine. The life that they lead is not the way I would choose to live," replied Tommy, and he then quickly changed the subject.

Nellie could not understand his feelings as she would have given anything to have known her mother, but because he appeared so emphatic about closing down the subject, she decided it would be wise to keep her thoughts to herself.

"Next Sunday, you are not working are you, Nellie?" asked Tommy.

"No, I am working on Saturday though, why is that?"

"I just thought that I might take you out somewhere nice."

"Do you want me to ask Connie and Pete to join us?" enquired Nellie.

"Not this time," said Tommy. "I do enjoy their company, but I thought it might be a nice change to be alone, if that's alright with you."

"Of course, where are we going then?"

"It's a secret," smiled Tommy.

So on the Sunday, Nellie got herself ready to go out. She wore a lemon dress which nipped in at her small waist then flared out, it had a white waist belt to contrast with white sandals to match. Nellie also wore a pair of white gloves. The weather was sunny and very warm, so Nellie took her hat to protect her face and a white cardigan, just in case the weather changed.

"The British weather can be so changeable," she muttered to herself.

"You look a million dollars," said Tommy as he lifted her up and gave her a long kiss when he saw her as she opened the front door to him. "I can see that I will need to hang on to you tightly otherwise some other guy will be whisking you away from me."

"Oh Tommy, you are a one, but thank you for the compliments," smiled Nellie as he gently put her back down. Grabbing her handbag, she called out her goodbyes to Mary.

"Going anywhere nice?" called out Mary from her lounge, as by now they had all become such close friends that the girls would often go into Mary's for a cup of tea.

"I don't know," said Nellie. "Tommy is taking me out for the day but he is being very secretive."

"Well, have a good time whatever it is you are doing."

"See you all later," Nellie called out as they made their way to the door.

Tommy remained very tight-lipped as to where they were going as they boarded the train into London. Firstly, they went to the Lyons Corner Tea House in the Strand where Nellie commented, "What is this big surprise? No offence, but this is more like a busman's holiday."

"Just be patient, you will see."

From there, they went on the train to Hyde Park which is one of London's biggest and best known parks.

"It is apparently one of Henry VIII's hunting grounds," explained Tommy as he was heading off in the direction of the lake.

The grounds looked absolutely fabulous, the trees were in full bloom and the flowers were all showing off their vibrant display of colours and perfumes.

Families were out and children were running around freely, chasing one another around the various shrubs, or playing ball with their parents. Babies that were just taking their first steps were clearly enjoying the sensation of grass under their feet.

"Well, my sweet, we are going for a row on the river."

Nellie, although surprised, agreed that it was the most perfect day to be on the river. She had never been in a boat before and was slightly concerned as she could not swim.

"You will be perfectly safe with me, I won't let you fall out and drown," laughed Tommy.

"Well, that's very reassuring."

Gradually, Nellie relaxed and with the gentle sound of the water lapping at the boat's sides, the sparkle on the river as the warm sun shone and the birds were singing to their hearts' content. Nellie felt that the day was just magical and hoped that it would never end. Tommy gently rowed the small boat along as they chatted about this and that and Nellie had to admire the fact he was quite skilled at manoeuvring the boat without causing any splashing.

"I am glad that we did not invite the others to join us," remarked Nellie, "just us two is just so romantic that I will remember today forever."

Tommy then found a spot along the bank which had a small gap between the shrubbery in which to pull alongside. He jumped out and tied the small boat up.

"Here, what are you up to, Tommy Brown?" said Nellie. "We will not have any hanky-panky going on."

"Trust me, Nellie," said Tommy a little seriously, "I do not have any such thoughts in my head, well, not at the moment anyway." He smiled and gave her a wink.

Nellie gingerly managed to get herself out and onto the bank and with no further ado, Tommy went down on one knee and proposed to a delighted and very surprised Nellie.

"That was totally unexpected, Tommy Brown."

"Well, please put me out of my misery and say something, preferably yes."

"Oh yes, yes, yes," she cried as Tommy then gently placed a ring on her finger.

For the rest of their outing, Nellie was unable to stop looking at her beautiful engagement ring.

During the journey home, Nellie felt that she was floating on air. The man she had fallen in love with on their first meeting was soon to be her husband and as she reflected on the day, it seemed that this was what fairy tales were made of. Nellie felt sure that their marriage would be a long and fruitful one, the bond was strong and with so much in common it surely could not fail to be a happy union.

When they arrived back in Bethnal Green and walked from the underground station to the house, it seemed to be unusually quiet.

"Strange," said Nellie, "I thought that Connie or Mary would be in. Oh well, I will make us a cup of tea and wait for them to return, I can't wait to give them our news."

"Congratulations!" was the shout from what appeared to be many voices.

There in the sitting room were her grandparents, Mary, Connie, Pete and Grace with tea, sandwiches and cakes all set out on the table.

"You all knew what Tommy had planned for the day then?" asked Nellie.

"Well, we did not know everything but Tommy had been and asked your granddad's permission to propose and suggested that it would be nice for us all to be here today for a surprise party, so we put two and two together and hoped for the best."

"Supposing I had declined Tommy's proposal?" said Nellie.

"Give over," replied Connie, "that was never going to happen, not the way you two are together. Come on, let's eat, we are all starving."

What a party they had!

The wedding was held in March 1939 and it proved to be a glorious day with the sun shining, although still a little chilly. Nellie had brought herself a beautiful cornflower blue suit which brought out the colour of her eyes and carried a small bouquet of spring flowers. Her grandmother had given her a delicate broach of a bouquet of pink and blue flowers set in silver which had belonged to Nellie's own mother, Nellie placed this very special gift on her suite jacket and felt the heat and the sting of tears in her eyes and said that she would be very proud to wear it.

"Your mum would have wanted you to have this on your wedding day as we gave it to her when she married your father. How proud your mum would have been today."

Mary gave Nellie a beautiful pair of cream lace gloves that she herself had worn only once and that was on her own wedding day. Connie and Grace, along with some work mates, clubbed together for a wedding reception. Nellie and Tommy had a small wedding with just their nearest and dearest and a few work friends with them to celebrate their day. Nellie's grandparents treated Tommy just like they would a son if they had been blessed with one and her grandfather commented that at last he would now have some male company with sensible conversations instead of just women's chatter to listen to.

Nellie was rather sad that Tommy's own parents did not attend, or even send a telegram of good wishes, but Tommy did not seem too bothered or concerned. Tommy just commented that events in Europe were building up and that it was not possible for them to leave where they were living. With this, the conversation changed as nothing was going to spoil Nellie and Tommy's day.

The honeymoon was just a week in a Bed and Breakfast in Southend-on-Sea in Essex and they promised themselves that one day when they were financially better off, they would treat themselves to somewhere perhaps slightly more exotic for a second honeymoon. During their week's honeymoon, they enjoyed walks along the sea front and sat watching the sun go down in the evenings just sitting along the promenade. Although money was tight and they were not able to splash out on anything fancy, fish and chips along the sea front had never tasted so good. They were in love and nothing else mattered.

Initially, the couple lived with Nellie's grandparents and everyone got on well; the older couple knew that the newlyweds needed some private space besides just their bedroom, so they changed the parlour (front room) into a small sitting room, but everything else was shared. Tommy and Granddad would often sit for a long time discussing the growing events in Europe and how things appeared to be gathering pace and that there was talk of ration books being printed in case they were needed in the future.

Everyone tried to get on with their normal lives but obviously things that were going on in Europe and with Germany were all very unsettling and tensions were mounting.

"I have some good news for you," said Nellie's nan when they arrived home that evening.

Nellie was now working her leave at Lyons Corner House, because as she was now a married lady she could not continue there.

"I have just heard that there is a house up for rent not too far from here in Plaistow, so if you are interested, then I suggest that you go along and see the landlord quickly before someone else nabs it."

As soon as Nellie saw the house, she instantly fell in love with it. It was everything that she could have wanted. From the outside, it was one property in from the end of a dead end turning with a detached house next door then an alleyway into the next street. The pathway at the front of the house had a flowering cherry tree just outside the front door which was now in full bloom, with masses of pink flowers. Trees also lined the pavements on both sides of the road which were just starting to show their buds all ready to burst into life.

"I bet that this turning looks an absolute picture in the summer!" exclaimed Nellie.

The house was a Victorian end of terrace property with bay windows downstairs, and the pathway to the front porch had black and white tiles. The inside of the house appeared to be huge to this young couple as it had two rooms downstairs and a scullery, two bedrooms upstairs and an outside toilet.

"Plenty of room for the kids when they come along," said Tommy.

"Give us a bleeding chance," replied Nellie. "Let's enjoy one another's company for a while."

"I say let's start now," as Tommy chased her up the stairs and into one of the bedrooms.

"Ah Gran, it is the cherry on the cake for me, I have so much to be thankful for and now a two-bedroom house, life could not get any better."

"I can't wait to see the house and help you and Tommy get settled," said her gran. "I will speak to friends and see if we can get a few bits and bobs together to help until you get your own things."

"It just needs a real good clean up and a lick of paint. I can put some lovely net curtains at the front bay windows and I bet with a good scrub those black and white tiles out the front will come up a treat. We will have our own little palace in no time," said Nellie.

So they soon were able to move into their own place and begin a new life together. On the day that they moved in with their few belongings, Tommy as is the tradition carried his wife over the threshold, which made Nellie giggle. Cobbled together by friends and neighbours, the young couple had some rudiments of furniture, cutlery and china. Tommy insisted that the one thing that they would have new was a bed, the sheets and blankets were a wedding gift by her now very dear friend Mary, who also would miss having Nellie around the house.

Nellie and Tommy held their first tea party with her grandparents and their friends to welcome them all to their new house. Nellie wanted to do everything herself, apart from making a cake which she was happy to delegate to her grandmother. The menfolk had nipped down to the local pub on the strict instructions of one pint only, leaving the women to prepare the tea. A new tablecloth was covering the table and although the chinaware was a mixture of colours and styles, somehow Nellie had made it look elegant and right, thanks to her training at the Lyons tea house. A small vase containing some dainty fresh flowers was placed on the table in the centre, a couple of chairs had been placed against one of the walls so that the older guests could sit down. Sandwiches and cakes, some of which had been supplied by her friends, were plentiful, and the cups of tea seemed to be endless. Once everyone had eaten as much as they could consume, the women began clearing everything away into the scullery ready to wash and dry the dishes. With this, the men suggested that they might just go down the road for one more pint so as not to be in the way!

When the men returned sometime later, everything was clean and tidy again and a couple more chairs were brought in from the parlour. Nellie was happy sitting on the lino-covered floor on a rag rug that her grandmother had made for her some years previously. After another cup of tea had been consumed, the guests made their departure with the promise that they would do it again soon.

"What a wonderful afternoon having everyone we love here with us in our own home, I think it went well and everyone certainly had plenty of food. In fact, there is enough cake to last the rest of the week."

"I am so proud of you and our house," said Tommy, "and like you, it was wonderful having our first guests, but what I love most is having you to myself. Now get up those stairs and we can celebrate in our own private way."

"Tommy Brown! It is still only the afternoon," laughed Nellie.

Chapter 4

Tommy had worked in the financial department at the local Tate and Lyle sugar factory since leaving school, he was a bright young man with a good head for figures and showed the potential to climb the ladder of success, but at the present he was still classed as a junior. His salary although not huge enabled the young couple to improve their little home gradually.

Nellie, who was now not working, filled her days with cleaning and polishing. Walls in most of the rooms had been whitewashed, small pictures graced the walls, vases with a few flowers, some even being colourful weeds, were in the parlour room at the front of the house and the main room where they generally sat. Windows and their sills were scrubbed within an inch of their life to remove the build-up of soot from the open fires which were in most rooms. Curtains were hanging in the windows which framed the sparkling glass. The black and white Victorian tiles that lead up the front path to the door gleamed as if they were brand new. The front door had also been treated to a thorough scrub and the brass knocker positively gleamed. Nellie was so proud of their house and her chest puffed up even more when the neighbours commented on it.

"Hey Nellie," called out Rosie, one of the neighbours. "Careful, gel, there's that much shine on them tiles that someone's gonna slip and fall on their bleedin' arse one of these days."

Nellie laughed. She had become very fond of some of her neighbours. They were often coarse, Tommy described them as 'rough diamonds', but these ladies did not have much, and what they had they would share. Not much went on in the street that they missed.

The young couple gradually settled into married life. Like all newlyweds, they had a few initial hiccups like the day Nellie decided to make a syrup sponge pudding. Nellie thought that Tommy might enjoy a sweet after dinner, so she prepared the syrup pudding as a surprise. That night, when Tommy arrived home from work and opened the front door, he was met with a delicious sweet smell wafting from the kitchen.

"Something smells good."

"I have made you a pudding," came the reply from the kitchen. "I have never made one before so I hope that it tastes OK."

"Well, judging by the aroma coming from the kitchen if it tastes as good as it smells, it will be delicious."

So after they had eaten the main course, with some ceremony, Nellie turned the pudding out onto the plate. Unfortunately, Nellie had mixed all the ingredients together, including the syrup, so instead of the pudding standing up proud with the syrup gently running down the sides of the sponge, it actually fell and spread across the plate in one sloppy mass. Tommy looked at Nellie, he dared not laugh and waited for her response.

"Bloody hell, it did not look like that when Nan made it!"

Now Tommy was unable to contain himself as he burst out laughing.

"I think that I need to find out from Nan how it is made before I try again."

"Never mind, Nellie, the thought was there." Then when Tommy heard the loud *plop* sound as it landed in the bin, he could not suppress his laughter. Seconds later, instead of feeling like she could cry after all her hard work, she too began to laugh until the tears rolled down her cheeks.

"Will custard do?" asked Nellie.

One day, when Nellie's grandmother visited, she asked Nellie if she would like a second-hand sewing machine.

"It belongs to one of my friends who no longer has any use for it and wondered if you would like it."

"Wow, would I!" replied an excited Nellie.

"It just fits nicely in the front parlour, especially with the light coming in that window," said her nan, "and it looks like new now you have given it a thorough clean-up."

There proudly stood the shiny black Singer treadle sewing machine with its gold writing.

"Oh Gran, I did not expect it to be such a wonderful machine. I will be able to make so much on it; the first thing I must make is a small thank you gift for your friend though, what do you think she might like?"

The house had a small garden which they both loved being in. Nellie kept a small area to grow some flowers which she would cut to display in vases in the house. Tommy took charge of growing some vegetables, runner beans, tomatoes etc and even made some space to grow a few potatoes.

"I shall have to look and see if there are any available allotments, then we would be able to grow so much more."

"Hey! What's with the we?" laughed Nellie.

Nellie and Tommy had got to know some of the neighbours in the street but mostly on a casual basis. As newlyweds, they were still very much enjoying each other's company, especially if Tommy had had a long day. On one side was Mrs Anderson, an elderly lady who only had one son who had a false leg, or so they presumed, judging by the why he walked, but as Mrs Anderson was a very quiet, gentle sort of a person and Nellie did not wish to appear nosey by asking questions. Nellie kept an eye out for the elderly lady, but would not intrude on her privacy Often though if they were in the garden at the same time, they would always have a chat over the fence.

"If ever you need any help, please do not hesitate to call me," said Nellie one day whilst chatting as they hung the washing out.

The neighbours on the other side were a different kettle of fish. There were the parents then two boys and two girls. The eldest boy had now left school and was working in the docks along with his father. Then there were the girls next, one training to be a hairdresser and the other still at school as was the youngest boy. They also tended to keep themselves to themselves, although as with most kids often the shout out of "Can we have our ball back please, Mrs Brown?" was heard from inside the house.

"That bloody ball spends more time in our garden than theirs and it smashes down some of my beautiful plants," grumbled Nellie one day when she had had enough.

"Give the lads a chance, Nell," replied Tommy. "If they play out in the street, people moan at them if the ball hits the windows or doors. One day, we may have a son and we will be on the other side of the argument, so let's try and be a little tolerant," said Tommy as he gave Nellie a little cuddle to settle her down.

"Well! Ain't they heard of a park?" Nellie needed to have the last word on the matter.

Further up the street were two sisters who lived side by side along with their husbands and grown up children. The women were much older than Nellie, but were friendly and would offer help and advice when Nellie needed someone to talk to if she was unable to go to visit her nan. The sisters generally got on very well, but now and then they would have a falling out and sometimes they could be heard having a real old ding dong with some colourful language thrown in for good measure whilst they were outside cleaning their windows or sweeping the pathway. But everyone knew that deep down the bond between them was very strong, and at your peril would you try to come between them. Not even their husbands dared to intervene.

Then there was the aforesaid Rosie who lived further up the street and her friend Marjorie Margi, as she was best known as, who lived in the next turning. These two were real characters and although not to everyone's taste, Nellie had a real soft spot for them. Nellie would get quite an education from these two when they got going.

One evening, during their first winter in their house, Nellie had gone up to their bedroom and quickly undressed and got into bed as the room was very cold. Often there would be almost as much ice on the inside of the windows as on the outside. As she snuggled down under the eiderdown, Tommy came in and jumped into bed.

"Bloody hell, Tommy, your feet and hands are freezing," she said as he tried to snuggle up close. "Get off, you old bugger, don't you dare come near me until you have warmed up a bit."

"I can show you a very quick way that we can both warm up," replied Tommy as he grinned at Nellie.

The Victorian houses did not have inside toilets but a small building on the outside of the house which was very basic. It had a wooden door which was open at the top and bottom with just a wooden seat and flushing chain, so a visit, especially in winter, was a very quick affair and often with only a candle to light the way.

Sunday nights were bath nights. They had an old tin bath that was kept outside hanging on some long nails in the wall. Nellie would heat up the water in her old copper which she used for washing her clothes in, then the water would be transferred into the tin bath, jug by jug. When the weather was really cold, they would put the bath in front of the living room open fire instead of the kitchen. This would be followed by hot chocolate and toast.

"This is the life," said Tommy, as they sat on their old second-hand sofa, snuggled up to one another in their dressing gowns.

The young couple loved their life so much; so it was very cold in the winter at times and going outside to the loo was no picnic, but it was theirs.

"One day," said Tommy, "we will be able to move away from here, have a bigger house with a big garden and a few more home comforts."

"Stop right there," said Nellie. "Let me tell you that I will never want to leave this house, I just love it so much. OK it can be very cold at times, but it has so much charm and character, good neighbours, close to the shops and most importantly, it is our first home filled with love and lots of fun. No, I do not think that I would ever want to move from here."

"So," replied Tommy, "I will ask you again in a few years' time when you have six kids running around your feet and only two bedrooms to share. Tommy then waited for the response he was expecting…"

"Who said anything about six kids!"

The humour and banter thus continued and long may this happiness last, hoped Nellie.

"We are so proud of the pair of you," said Nellie's grandparents on one of their visits.

Often they would have their Sunday dinner at Nellie and Tommy's house and her grandmother would continue to teach Nellie recipes which she would try out, much to Tommy's delight; syrup sponge and spotty dick were firm favourites and they would often have a good laugh when they remembered the earlier attempts. Nellie kept in touch with her friends Connie, Grace and Mary, but she was no longer working at the tea rooms as per their terms and conditions of employment so they met up less frequently. On one occasion, the young couple had invited Connie and her now boyfriend Pete over for dinner. The girls had made an effort to dress up as they used to when going out for the evening.

"Wow, you girls look fabulous!" Pete exclaimed, unable to take his eyes off of Connie.

"We always look fabulous," replied the girls in unison.

From here on, the evening was just so relaxed, they were all just comfortable in one another's company.

They would often go to local dances as a foursome and listen and dance to the latest bands. Connie's relationship with Pete was now very strong and Nellie would often tease Connie.

"Ain't he proposed to you yet, what's he waiting for?"

"Give over, Nellie, we have both decided to wait for a while."

One Saturday, the girls had managed to persuade the men to take them to the local hall for a dance. The girls had each put their hair up in rollers in the morning and for the rest of the day wore scarves over their heads. In the evening, they had got together at Nellie's house to apply their makeup and brush one another's hair and put it up into the latest fashionable style. Once dressed in their seamed stockings and dresses, they both really did look a treat.

"Here," said Tommy to Pete, "do you reckon that these two have dressed up like this for our sake, or the band playing tonight?"

"You know that we only have eyes for you two," replied Nellie as she gave Connie a sneaky wink.

"I saw that, Nellie Brown," replied Tommy as he put his arms around his woman's waist.

They all had a grand evening dancing, it felt good to have some fun together every now and again, especially as the talk of possible war was never far away.

Nellie and Connie had now moved on to drinking port and lemon which after their earlier experiments with alcohol, seemed to suit them more; neither wanted to repeat their earlier experience.

"How are Mary and Grace?" asked Nellie. "I feel really bad that I have not been over to see them in ages."

"Mary is unchanged, she has never let your room out since you left. She feels that bringing someone else in might upset the apple cart, but I told her that if she needs the rent then she has to. I am sure that we would get on with someone new, but she says that she is fine at the moment. As for Grace, well, she appears to be getting serious with her boyfriend. Canadian I think she said he was and there has even been talk that he has to go back home soon and that Grace is thinking of going with him."

"That is very brave or stupid of her if she has only known him for a short time and knows nothing about his family or home life."

"We have told her that and suggested she just wait for a while, but she seems adamant, so we shall just have to wait and see nearer the time," replied Connie.

Unease was building in Europe but the couple tried not to dwell on the subject for too long.

"How about going to the pictures tonight, Nell? There is a new film out called 'The Wizard of Oz'. We haven't had a night out in ages."

"I would like that, shall we just have some pie and mash for dinner, save cooking?" replied Nellie.

The pair did enjoy pie and mash which was an East End favourite.

"I do not know how you can now eat popcorn after that dinner, Tommy," said Nellie.

"It's traditional, you have to have popcorn while watching a film. Now sit back and enjoy the film," replied Tommy.

"I really enjoyed tonight, thank you," said Nellie.

"It is good to have a treat now and again," said Tommy, "especially with what is going on at the moment."

"Let's not talk about that now, please do not spoil this evening. We will go home and have some hot cocoa and toast and worry about tomorrow when tomorrow comes."

But tomorrow may come quicker than we would like, thought Tommy.

The dark cloud that had been hanging over the nation and Europe was now beginning to gather pace.

"You don't think that there will be another war, do you, Granddad?" asked Nellie on one of her visits.

"No, lass, no one wants to go to war again. Neville Chamberlain believes that war should be avoided at all costs and negotiations are on-going."

But Chamberlain had promised Poland that Britain would come to its aid if Germany invaded them. Nellie tried hard to put from her mind the worries and concerns that were building up.

Conversations especially amongst the men were generally on the subject. Nellie desperately wanted the issues to go away and tried distraction methods for her and Tommy. They would often go for walks in the evening and sometimes at the weekend, they would go to Canning Town Station then on to Woolwich Park for the day, often taking a picnic with them and while away many an hour. Other times, they would get a train and go off to Southend-On-Sea where they had spent a week on their honeymoon.

"One day, when we have the money, I will give you a proper honeymoon. Maybe we could go to Yorkshire or get the train up to Scotland, but for sure I will make it up to you."

"So long as I have you, I have no need for any exotic holidays. I love the East End and my house, I have everything that I need and want around me now."

Nellie did not know it but one day, she would sadly reflect on these treasured moments. But the possibility of war with Germany would not go away.

Hitler invaded Poland on 1 September. Two days later, on the 3rd, Nellie and Tommy had gone to her grandparents for Sunday dinner. Outside some of the neighbours were cutting their small patches of lawn in their gardens then at 11.15 am, everyone's life as they knew it was about to change. Lawn mowers went off, children's voices playing seemed to silence and the radios went on.

Neville Chamberlain broadcasted to the nation:

"The German Government had been handed a final note that if they did not withdraw troops by 11 am, then a state of war would exist between them." He continued, "No such undertaking was taken and so now Britain is at war with Germany."

This radio broadcast was then minutes later followed by the sound of the air raid sirens. It was a false alarm but it was now war and the nation needed to get used to the sound of the siren as there would be many more to follow.

Everyone just sat in disbelief. They all had hoped that such an event would be averted and that a solution would be found.

Tommy and Nellie walked home from her grandparents' who lived in Canning Town almost all the way in stunned silence. They did not notice if it was still sunny or raining.

The already printed ration booklets were issued to the public on 8 Sept, just five days after war was declared.

In the New Year of 1940, rationing was introduced, but little happened in Western Europe until the spring.

Chapter 5

"Oh your poor flower patch," said Tommy as Nellie started to clear the ground ready to put in their air raid shelter.

"Never mind, at least we may be safer in the shelter than staying inside looking at pretty flowers," replied Nellie.

She was so upset as her flowerbed, that by now was producing some lovely blooms, had to be dug up. Tommy explained to Nellie that once the Anderson shelter had been dug into the ground and covered with three feet of soil as advised, then they would be better off continuing to grow as many vegetables as the ground allowed, as he explained, "Now that everything is going to be rationed, it makes sense to grow our own. I also think it will be worth us getting a couple of chickens and making a coup so at least we may get some eggs."

Everyone had been educated to recognise the sounds of the siren and when to take cover and then the all-clear, when the siren was intermittent, that represented the time to get to the nearest shelter and the all-clear would be a continuous sound.

"Bloody hell, when the siren goes off, it puts the fear of god into us. Will we ever get used to it and let's hope it does not happen too often." This was the general consensus of the women in the street.

Gas masks were also introduced for fear of being gassed, everyone was advised to keep them with them at all times and were to be carried in the box over their shoulder by the strap as supplied. Babies and children were also provided with gas masks which were often made of bright colours so they appeared less frightening. Young babies were totally enclosed and the air was pumped into the mask with a hand pump.

"If the gas rattles sound then everyone should put on their masks immediately, even if you are in bed," was the advice given.

"I hate those things," moaned Nellie, "they stink of rubber and when you try and talk, it sounds like you are farting all the time."

"Better that than being gassed," replied Tommy.

"Yea, mind you when you fart, Tommy Brown, that's when I need to wear the gas mask."

True to the London spirit that was to prevail, they had a jolly good laugh.

People by the spring of 1940 had generally stopped wearing the masks as the fear of being gassed did not materialise.

Nellie's grandparents also had a shelter in their garden.

"I do worry about them two," said Nellie. "They don't move as fast as they used to, what if they don't get to the shelter in time and they get blown up?"

"Now then, my love, I am sure that we will be given plenty of warning and time to get to cover before the attacks start. I am sure that they will be fine."

Initially not much happened and children that had previously been evacuated to the country for their safety were brought back home by their parents, only to be evacuated again later on.

Many things were changing around the young couple. Blackout curtains were required to be hung at the windows as no lights were allowed to be seen from outside, wardens would patrol the streets to ensure that no chinks of light were showing. Rationing came into force.

"It's just as well, I needed to lose some weight," joked Nellie one day, as she like many women had to learn new ways of cooking to make food go further. "It must be so hard for families, thank god we don't have any kids, that's not for the want of trying, but for that I am thankful, especially when you see those poor kids and mums having to say goodbye to each other at the stations not knowing when or even if they would be together again."

"I think that I will go and see how the girls are getting on in Bethnal Green and see how they are managing. I do worry as they are closer to London than we are," said Nellie anxiously.

"Give them all my love and tell them to take care," came the equally concerned reply from Tommy.

"We are absolutely fine here," said Connie and Mary.

"Where is young Grace?" asked Nellie.

"She has gone," said Connie with a slightly angry tone to her voice.

"What do you mean gone?"

"We got up one morning a week ago to find a note in her room to say that she has left for Canada with her gentleman friend. There was no forwarding address, so we do not have a clue when she went or where. Poor Mary, she is so concerned for her safety. You know how she sees herself as responsible for us," continued Connie.

"How ungrateful and silly can she be," said Nellie. "In these uncertain times, she does not have a clue what may be in store for her."

"Let's hope that she does not live to regret her hasty decision," added Mary.

"Anyway, how are you and Tommy managing?" Connie asked. "It seems like ages since we last saw one another. We need to arrange a night out again, how about the pictures, there are a few good films out at present," said Connie.

"Sit down, Nellie, we need to talk."

Tommy's face looked very serious. Nellie's heart began to beat a little faster and she felt sick.

"I have applied to join the navy. I have to do my bit for the country and our future, Nell, and I want to choose which service I join and not wait until I am told. You do understand, don't you, my love?"

"I do understand but I don't have to like it. When did you decide all this then?"

"Pete and I have discussed it many a time lately. He wishes to join the army, so we met up the other day and we both went along and joined up. I am sorry that I did not discuss it with you first, but I knew that you would try and talk me out of it. I have to do this, Nellie, please understand."

"Bloody hell, Tommy!" Nellie screamed as the tears rolled down her cheeks with both anger and fear gripping her. "We have only been married five minutes and you are leaving me. I hate this bloody war already and how rapidly it is changing our lives."

Tommy just sat and held Nellie until she settled down again.

"Does Connie know?"

"I believe that Pete is going to tell her today as well. We thought that way neither of you would have to keep a secret from the other."

Nellie did eventually have to respect and accept that this was a major decision that Tommy had made and it could not have been an easy one and for that, she was immensely proud of him and loved him all the more for it. She knew that this was something that if the war continued then many other men would be making the same decision, but she just wished it was not happening so soon. If you have to fight then at least do it in the forces of your choice.

"I am so scared, Tommy, what if something happens? If you are injured or worse and I am not there with you?"

"I know, my love, but believe me I have no wish to die just yet either. Let's try to be positive, it is done now so let's enjoy this time together before I am called to start my training."

Both girls cried when they met up; the men that they loved dearly were going away to fight for king and country.

"What shall we do without them?" cried Nellie, tears rolling down and leaving tear streaks down her cheeks.

"Well, we have to respect their decision; after all, they are putting on a brave face for us, but they must be scared of what may be, so we have to be strong and supportive for them and not let them see us crying. If they are strong of mind, then so must we be, then when they leave to fight, then so must we find work to help the war effort as well." Connie desperately tried to sound strong, accepting and confident, but inside her heart was breaking.

"You will never guess what," said Connie one day shortly after the men had informed them of their plans to join the services. "He has only gone and proposed to me and I have accepted."

"About 'bloody' time!" smiled Nellie as she gave Connie a huge embrace. "Congratulations to you. What has made him ask you now?"

"Pete says that now that there is a war on and that he is going away, he would like to go in the knowledge that he has a wife waiting for him back home."

So wedding plans, although small and hurried, would now be planned with Nellie being a bridesmaid and Tommy the best man.

Connie contacted her family back in Ireland; they were delighted for her and were sad that they had not got to meet Pete. Her parents had not even ventured out of their little village that they had lived in since they had married so they would not be attending the wedding but wished them both well. They hoped that when the troubles were over, they would go over to them for a visit. Connie's older sister also sent her best wishes, but again was unable to attend, and hoped that peace would not be too far away then they would be able to reunite again and celebrate in style. Connie would obviously have liked to have her family attend her wedding but accepted that in these times it was not really feasible.

"Well, if Tommy is to be the best man, then he can't give you away, so would you like Granddad to step in? After all, he has known you for a few years now," asked Nellie.

"I would like that very much, then after this blooming war I would like a blessing in the Catholic church back home with my family."

Connie, Nellie, Mary, Agnes, all went out to find an outfit for the wedding. Rationing was now in force so the choice was very restrictive. Nellie by chance was able to obtain some parachute silk from someone who knew someone at the local market; there was just sufficient to make a wedding dress. Fortunately, Connie was quite petite so not too much fabric was required.

"It is fabulous, you are so clever, Nellie!" exclaimed Connie as she tried her dress on and looked at herself in the mirror. "Now I will feel like a real bride."

The dress was not a full flouncy willowy kind of dress, but a slim, slightly fitted style and Nellie had managed to find a few small beads from old clothes that she had rummaged. Also, friends of Agnes had given some trinkets from their button boxes to help embellish the bridal dress.

Many women had button boxes that were filled with old buttons, trinkets and lace that had been removed from previous garments, which during the war time with the make do and mend attitude became very useful.

Carrying a small bouquet of fresh flowers, with hair and makeup carried out by Nellie, Connie looked fabulous. The other guests, including Nellie, wore clothes that they already had. Nellie wore the outfit she had worn for her own wedding and she was delighted that it fitted as good as it had then. The wedding reception was held at Mary's house which was where Connie had still been living and everyone had contributed some food, mainly sandwiches, and the wedding cake made by Mary was an iced sponge cake which looked spectacular, but was really a sponge cake covered with an iced cardboard cover which had been borrowed from the baker. It had been placed over the sponge to give the impression of a large fancy wedding cake, but the bride and groom could not care, to them the day was perfect.

After the small reception consisting of the bride and groom, Nellie, Tommy, Mary and Nellie's grandparents, they all went along to the local pub and had a good old knees up, hoping that the sirens would not go off upsetting a perfect day.

A few weeks later, the letter that Nellie dreaded arrived and hit the door mat with what Nellie felt sounded like a clap of thunder.

"Well, this is it," said Tommy as he opened the letter and read down the page. "I start my training in a week's time. I have to report to 'Shotley, *HMS Ganges*' at 9 am on the Monday morning, ready to start my six weeks of training."

"Bloody hell, Tommy, that has come round quicker than I had hoped. It only seems like five minutes ago that you signed up."

Time went so fast, Nellie wished that she could have stopped all the clocks and generally stop time so that they could remain in their own little bubble, but life is not like that and the time was near to say their goodbyes.

On the Sunday before Tommy was due to leave, they went to dinner at her grandparents' in order that they may say their goodbyes and wish Tommy well. Nellie whilst in the kitchen with her grandmother shed a few tears.

"Now then, lass, stop that and wipe your eyes. As difficult as it is for you both, you have to be strong for one another," soothed her grandmother. "Try to keep your emotions under control for a short time longer."

Nellie went along with her husband to the station, where there appeared to be hundreds of other couples. The men were kissing their wives and sweethearts and then getting onto the train. From there, they were competing to get to the open windows to wave their last goodbyes. Then as the train pulled away from the station, with arms still hanging out, it quickly disappeared from view leaving behind a smoke-filled station. People then started to depart from the platform; mums, dads, wives and girlfriends all with their own lives and homes to return to, each experiencing the same emotions of fear and anxiety. Although Tommy would be home on leave for a short period after his training, there were many on the platform who were returning to fight and may never return home.

Leaving the station, Nellie was quite aware that the man she loved more than life itself would be home again in a few weeks' time, but the next time she stood on the same platform would be a totally different experience.

Not feeling up to visiting anyone, Nellie made her way straight home. As she opened the front door, the quietness, coldness and emptiness hit her like a hammer blow and she began to cry like she would never stop.

Nellie kept herself busy whilst Tommy was training, she would pop to her grandparents' three or four times a week, run errands for them and do a bit of tidying up. Age was starting to show now; they were getting slow and they both slept quite a bit.

"I do worry about the pair of you now, won't you come and live with me? I have lots of space and I could cook for you and do your washing so that you two can take life easy. Even though we are supposed to be at war, nothing has been happening for a while now, perhaps it won't."

"Thank you so much, my love, but if I had nothing to do all day to keep me busy, then I might as well be dead. Thank you for your kind thought but truly we are fine and anyway, Tommy will soon be home from his training then you will want the house to yourselves," replied her nan.

Nellie knew from before that the look that her granny gave her now, although kindly, was a look that would brook no argument and not to continue with the subject, so Nellie smiled to herself and decided to leave it until another time.

Tommy was due home in just a few days' time, so Nellie cleaned the house from top to bottom, the sheets were clean and aired. Saving some of her coupons and going without some things, she was able to make a cake which was in the larder waiting to be consumed and she had been able to squirrel away a few favourite treats for Tommy's homecoming. Although she realised that it would only be for a brief time, she fully intended to make the most of it.

Brief it certainly was. It felt to Nellie that someone had sneaked in and put all the clocks and time forward, cheating them out of time together and on their last day, Nellie tried hard not to dwell on the things like when they were eating breakfast it may be a long time before they did it again. She desperately wanted to catch every last thing they did together and squeeze it into a bottle, so she could take it out again and again to relive it in the future.

"Where will you go to, and on what ship?" asked Nellie, wanting, yet not wanting to know or how long he would be gone for.

"I have to go to Chatham Naval Base and then await to be allocated a ship and then from there who knows."

"Nellie, I have been thinking, I would prefer it if you did not see me off at the station this time, I would rather say goodbye here in our own home. You know just how much I love you and that I wished with all my heart that this was not happening."

"But why?"

"Because it would feel more like I was just going off to work and I will be back later at tea time. I think it would be more bearable this way, I would rather have the picture in my mind of you waving me off from the front door than at the station."

Tommy obviously did not come home at tea time.

Nellie felt at a loss and very unsettled for a while, she did not wish to work just now as she felt that her grandparents, although they may have disagreed, really needed her close in these very unsettling times. So with Tommy now gone, she stayed with them for a time. It also helped to fill her day doing odd jobs for them. Weeks turned to months and all appeared to be strangely quiet. Nellie had returned back to her own place after a few weeks and was getting used to being on her own again.

"Let's go and see the film *Casablanca starring Humphrey Bogart and Ingrid Bergman*, it is supposed to be really good," suggested Connie on one occasion when the girls fancied going out. "How about going on Friday to the matinee showing, then going on for a quick drink in the nearby pub?"

"Connie, do you remember our first drinking experience?" laughed Nellie.

"I certainly do!" exclaimed Mary, who although older than the other two remained a very close friend. "The commotion you girls made when you came home thinking you were being quiet."

Most times when Nellie visited her grandparents and always on Sundays, they would sit and listen to the radio. Most people had a radio or gramophone, the BBC radio was the main form of home communication and entertainment.

"If it was not for the radio keeping us entertained with news and information as well as the comedy shows, I would have to listen to your gran all day going on about what is now being rationed," laughed Grandad.

"I can hear you," came a voice from the kitchen.

Nellie loved them both so much. Even after so many years of marriage, they could still bounce off one another in good humour.

It was now almost six months since war had been declared and there had been almost no fighting or bombing. It was now being called the Phoney War, but at least this time gave the government more time to protect Britain from an attack. Barrage balloons could be seen in the sky, which Nellie was informed were to make the Luftwaffe fly high when they were going to attack. Sandbags were piled 'round shops and public building entrances. Blackout curtains had already been enforced and by law every window had to be blacked out as not even a chink of light could be seen, allowing the enemy bombers any form of guidance.

Street lights were switched off or dimmed with shields over so that the light would be shone downwards, vehicles that were out had to be fitted with slotted covers to deflect the headlights downwards. Everywhere was now very dark and there were many accidents and fatalities. Going out onto the streets had become a very hazardous pastime, men were encouraged to wear their white shirt tails hanging out so that they could be seen by cars with dipped headlights.

Nellie visited Connie and Mary late one afternoon. It had already started to get dark and so was more difficult to navigate, so much so that she missed a pavement and twisted her ankle. "Bugger that!" said Nellie as she limped her way to her friends. After Pete had left to commence his duties in the army, Connie had decided that she would continue living at Mary's. It suited them both and made a lot of sense to share.

"Hello, ladies, how are you both?"

"Well, not too much has happened with this war yet, I am glad to say. Where will you both have to go for shelter if the bombing starts?" enquired Nellie on one of her regular visits.

"Oh Nellie, I realise that you are only joking, but we must not wake the sleeping dragon. I find this waiting to see if anything is going to happen more frightening," replied Connie.

Mary explained that they had to go down to the local underground station onto the platforms and stay there until the all-clear siren sounded. When the sirens go off, people from all around make their way there where they then would go down and squeeze in to find a place to sit.

"That should be nice and cosy with hundreds of others down there as well, you would be like moles," laughed Nellie, "but at least hopefully safe. Mind you, I thought that the government were not going to allow that, people on the underground."

"Ah well, it has now been agreed. What about you and your plans?" enquired Mary.

Nellie went on to tell them that she would use the Anderson shelter that she and Tommy had erected and that during the air raids she would run in the garden and take cover. Nellie also told them that she had offered to remove the fencing between her and her elderly neighbour so that she could use it as well.

"But bless her," said Nell, "she explained to me that she would take her chances in the house and that if she was blown up, then she would at last be with her husband and that is the first time that she has ever mentioned him."

The women then generally had a good catch up on any gossip.

"Have either of you ever heard from Grace, did she even arrive safely?" asked Nellie.

"Not a 'dickie bird', absolutely nothing," replied Connie. "You would have thought that after Mary's care and kindness, she would have contacted us."

"I am just worried that something has gone wrong and I can only hope that she is safe," said Mary. "Well, there is nothing that we can do now. Maybe one day, she may contact us again and let us know that all is well."

"Please come and live with me," pleaded Nellie on one of her visits to her grandparents. "I feel that something may be happening soon and I would rather we all be together."

Her grandparents were reluctant to leave their home, which they had lived in pretty much all their married life.

"We stand as much chance of being bombed there as here," said her granddad. "Anyway, lass, we have had a good life up until now and we are getting rather old and tired."

"But I love you both so very much, it would make me feel so much happier if I have you with me. There is plenty of space for you now that Tommy is away."

"Tell you what," said her granddad, "if it would make you feel better and stop you nagging us, how about if we pack up a few belongings and this weekend we come and stay for a while?"

"Thank you, Granddad, it really would make me feel happier and it will be company for me. I must confess that I am finding it quite lonely in that house on my own and if I am honest, I am scared of the thought of an air raid starting. I will come back tomorrow and help you to pack up and then I will start to take things back to my place and get it ready for you. It will be like old times again."

Nellie was never to see her beloved grandparents again.

That night, the Luftwaffe commenced the heavy bombing raids over London that would be known as the 'Blitz' and Nellie's grandparents' house and street took a direct hit, wiping out everything, as if they had never even existed.

The same evening when the sirens sounded, Nellie picked up her book, blankets and torch, then headed off into the Anderson shelter. Her heart was beating so fast, she felt as though it had moved into her ears. Even though she had prepared for this moment, this was the first time the sirens were for real.

Shortly after getting into the shelter, she heard the explosions, the planes, real and terrifying, the sounds, the lighting up of the sky, because even being in the shelter, through the small cracks and openings, the bright external lights entered. Smells of burning started to enter in through the gaps of the hut. Nellie tried not to focus on the sounds that were outside and she picked up her book, but that was of no comfort or distraction. She had never felt so frightened or alone in her life. She felt the bile from her stomach rising to her throat, just as she thought she could not hold back from being physically sick, she heard the sound of screaming and crying outside, then in through the entrance to the shelter burst the children and woman from next door.

"Jesus Christ!" screamed Nellie as she thought she was about to pass out not knowing who or what was entering the shelter. "What the hell are you doing bringing the kids out whilst bombs are dropping?"

The children were absolutely terrified, it took quite a time to stop them screaming and crying. Cuddling the children and wrapping them in the blanket and reassuring them prevented Nellie thinking about her own terror.

"I hope that you don't mind but me 'usband felt that me and the kids would be safer in 'ere with you, we was all bleedin' terrified when the sound of the bombs could be heard as it all sounds very close."

Nellie was actually glad of the company and having the children so petrified made her stronger and more able to calm down for their sakes, and not panic them. Sounds of the planes flying nearby, the wailing of the sirens, the scream of falling bombs mingling with the thump of gunfire, anti- aircraft guns could be heard. The skies were lit by clusters of parachute flares, which would illuminate areas being attacked, and the ringing bells of the fire brigade soon followed. These new sights and sounds that filled the air were beyond frightening. Nellie had initially called out to her elderly neighbours to come to the shelter, but the noise from the sirens probably drowned out her voice. Nellie just hoped that they were safe. The night continued on and the bombing was relentless.

"That explosion sounded really close, sounds like the docks are getting a 'ammering tonight," one of the neighbours' sons advised, causing Nellie's stomach to lurch and increased her anxiety about her grandparents and friends.

Stomach churning over and adrenaline rushing around her body was making her feel really sick. At one point, she actually contemplated going outside to throw up, but managed to suppress it again.

"Please, God, keep everyone safe tonight."

They remained in the shelter for the whole of the night. The children managed to get some sleep, but the two women remained awake and kept talking unless the noise was so loud that they could not hear one another.

"I am scared to go out there this morning, scared as to what we might find," said Nellie as the daylight sneaked in through the small holes in the shelter.

"Come on, gel, let's go and face the demons. At least we was safe," replied Jean the neighbour.

"It's funny," said Nellie, "I didn't have a clue to your name or you mine prior to last night."

"Yeh! That's what community spirit in the face of adversity does for you."

As the women and children came out and into the daylight, the acrid smell and smoke filled the air, but they were all surprised to see that their houses were all still standing, but as they looked up, smoke was reaching into the sky from all around them.

"Bad night last night, gels," said Jean's husband as he came out of the house where he had remained during the raid, staying under the large kitchen table. "A lot of areas around 'ere copped it, I reckon, we was very lucky. Kids OK, are they?"

The fear and anxiety that had lain dormant for a while in the pit of Nellie's stomach now came up to her throat and this time, she could not suppress it. Grabbing her coat, she ran to her grandparents' house, which was at least three miles away from her. Bombed out buildings and properties on fire, bells of the overworked fire crews rang in her ears, pipes presumably gas were belching out flames from areas that were once homes. People were walking looking dazed and disbelieving of what was in front of their eyes. An acrid smell pervaded the air, which made Nellie feel sick. People were scrabbling in the rubble trying to find any possessions that might be retrieved from what was left of their homes, others were wailing uncontrollably as the realisation of lost loved ones hit them. Curtains that were once someone's pride and joy were left blowing in the wind and smoke-filled air from windows that were clinging onto remnants of brickwork. Only young boys appeared to see it as an adventure and were looking for pieces of shrapnel to build up a collection and boast to other boys of their finds. Fear was now gripping Nellie as she neared where her grandparents lived.

As Nellie approached what was once her grandparents' street, she heard a loud scream. She was in so much shock that she was unaware that the sound had come from her own mouth. Running around over the rubble which was still unstable and in many places still alight, she was looking for anything that existed from her grandparents. Whistles were sounding and voices shouting, but Nellie was oblivious that they were for her. Scrabbling around and pulling at the brickwork with her own bare hands, she was oblivious to the fact that her hands and feet were bleeding badly, all she could hear was a wailing sound like that of a distressed animal not realising that it was herself.

"Take it easy, sweetheart, just rest."

Where was the sound coming from, was she dreaming, had it all been a terrible nightmare? As Nellie gradually opened her eyes, there holding her hand and stroking her head were Connie and Mary.

"Was it real, did I imagine it all, how did I get here?" all the questions just exploded from Nellie's mouth.

"Oh Nellie, we are so sorry for your loss. No, you did not dream it all. Your poor grandparents would not have known a thing, they would not have suffered; the bombings and explosions were so severe that they obliterated vast areas of London and the surrounding areas. Someone who recognised you brought you here, they said that you really needed to go to hospital to have your wounds attended to, but we wanted to look after you."

Nasty cuts to Nellie's hands and feet from walking over glass, pieces of timber and brick had been cleaned and dressed, preventing them from becoming infected. Her nails and tips of fingers were shredded where she had been scratching through the rubble, searching. Injuries that could be cleaned and dressed were done so, but the haunted look that was masking Nellie's beautiful face was not so easy to fix.

"She will need to stay with us for some time, I feel," said Mary. "She doted on her grandparents and the loss of them will be almost unbearable for her."

Nellie almost slept herself into oblivion. When the raids were on and the girls had to get down to the shelter, Nellie walked with them but it was robotic, she did not appear to be aware of anything around her; it was if her brain had completely shut down. Nellie remained in this state of shock for almost a week.

"Why, oh why did I not insist on taking them back with me sooner?" cried Nellie, as now the awful reality was sinking in.

"No one could have known that it was going to be so bad that first night, Nellie. You cannot blame yourself," soothed Connie.

But there was nothing to be said that would stop Nellie from ever blaming herself. She wept for the loss of them and for the fact that she was unable to say goodbye to them both and tell them that she loved them dearly.

Chapter 6

"I am so grateful you are both still alive, it seems that the closer that we are to London the worse it is," said Nellie.

"Last night was certainly a bad one, I thought that the bombing would never stop. The docks are an obvious target as is bombing the city of London. Apparently, St Paul's Cathedral is another target as it is such an iconic building, but if Hitler thinks he can break the London spirit, then he is misguided," Mary replied with a fierce determination.

Prior to the outbreak of war, Mary had purchased a radiogram. Often the girls would sit and listen to some music, or some of the comedy programs.

"Why don't you stay over for a couple of nights, Nellie, we can have a glass of something and enjoy an evening like old times," suggested Mary.

"Oh please, say yes," pleaded Connie, "it would be wonderful just to chat for an evening as we used to."

"Well, I suppose I could, it is not like I have to rush home for anything. Plus the fact I do not like to be out on the streets when it is dark."

"Sod off, Hitler, will you give us a break for once?" moaned Mary as the air raid sirens went off again during their evening together.

"Well, here we go again, get your things and Nellie, in that cupboard there you will find some blankets, grab them please. We need them to keep us warm down there on the station platform. Right then, let's get out of here and head for the shelter, don't forget your masks, girls," continued Mary, who still saw herself as the responsible adult.

Nellie had to admit to herself that the two women had the evacuation plan well under control and was impressed at the speed in which they worked, vacating the building grabbing everything that they may require as they went.

Nellie had not yet experienced being in the underground station during a raid before. "Bloody hell, I did not fully realise that it would be so packed down here."

"You'll get used to it, Nellie. It's not so bad compared to what shelter some have got. We can also have fun; some nights, we have a sing song, some entertain us with musical instruments and often others even if they only have spoons to play will join in. We all try to keep one another's spirits up as best we can. Also, it is less frightening for the children if the adults appear relaxed," advised Mary in her usual stoic way.

"So long as you don't have a snoring, farting old geezer, or woman come to that, right next to you," quipped Connie.

They all had a good laugh as they made their way down the steps onto the platform below.

Nellie stayed at Mary's for some time. The bombings continued and things were getting worse for the nation. Shortages of food and clothing were increasing so the girls all put their ration coupons together to try and make things go further. Nellie had like everyone else good days and bad days, but the girls also had fun, if you could call it that, by trying to copy some of Marguerite Patten's war time recipes.

"What the bloody hell is that supposed to be?" as a plate of food was put in front of the girls.

"It is a meat pie minus the meat," said Nellie.

"I am not so sure that it even resembles a pie," laughed Connie. "I thought that your nan had taught you how to cook."

Off went the sirens again. "You would think that by now we would be used to that sound, but it still gives me the shivers when it goes off," said Connie as they gathered a few belongings to take with them. "Grab your blankets again, everyone, we may be in for a long night of it."

Nellie returned to her own home after a few days. Although she enjoyed the company of the girls, especially after her recent loss, she was desperate to check if her own place had survived the bombings.

Nellie had kept all the letters from Tommy wrapped up in a red piece of ribbon with a bow on top. Sometimes, when she did not have time to read them, she would just take them out of the drawer in her bedroom and smell them, as they somehow gave her some comfort. Other times, she would read them again and again, absorbing what information he had been able to give her as if reading them for the first time. Nellie sent a letter on a weekly basis, telling him of things that had gone on. She made the decision not to tell him about the loss of her grandparents, as she was concerned that he would then worry as to how she was coping and that there was nothing he could do to help, so she decided that she would inform him on his next leave. Tommy's letters were pretty infrequent, not because they were not written, but often due to a long delay in them being posted, but she would have to be content in the knowledge that all was well.

After an exhausting period of heavy bombing, the girls decided to attend a dance that was being held in a local church hall.

"I feel that we need to have something to look forward to in these uncertain dreary times," suggested Connie.

Mary was not so keen. "You girls go and have a lovely time, I will be happy sitting and listening to my radio. Perhaps next week, we could go to the pictures, I would like to go and see that new film 'Gone with the Wind' with Clark Gable and Vivian Leigh; it is supposed to be really good."

"That's settled then, we shall do that, so long as you do not mind us two going out?" asked Connie.

"Not at all, you girls need to let your hair down and enjoy yourselves."

When the girls arrived at the dance hall, they could hear the band playing and lots of voices inside laughing and chatting away.

"Sounds as though there is a good turn out tonight."

"Well, let's face it, we all need to have some fun and enjoy ourselves. None of us know what is 'round the corner."

Inside the hall, there appeared to be many servicemen; some in uniform others in mufti. Women had made an effort to make themselves up; hair was in the latest fashion and because stockings were almost impossible to obtain, many with the aid of an eye liner pencil managed to draw a line up the backs of their legs to represent the line in the back of the stockings. Some had managed a straighter line than others. Everyone was making the most of the night out and the dance floor was never empty.

"Jesus, Connie, there are some goings on outside this building I can tell you. I just went to use the toilet and some sights that met my eyes would curl your hair."

"I am not saying that it is right," replied Connie, "but I suppose for some of the men, they don't know when or if they will be home again. Times are very different now than in peacetime."

"Well, I for one will be keeping my drawers on tight, no man other than my Tommy will see tomorrow's washing." Both girls then burst out laughing. "As my nan would say, 'Keep your hand on your happeney, girl'."

Christmas was not far away and both girls were hoping that the men would be on leave, but it was looking less likely the nearer they got.

"Stay with us until after Christmas," said Mary.

"Well, I must admit that being in an empty house for Christmas does not really hold any appeal, so thank you, I would like to stay."

Decorations were made out of strips of paper and turned into paper chains and they made some home-made crackers and managed to buy small gifts or find items in the rummage sales. Nellie being particularly clever with a needle and thread managed to find a candlewick bed spread in the second-hand stall and turn them into dressing gowns for Mary and Connie. Christmas dinner consisted of rabbit pie with roast potatoes and they had managed to get some carrots, this was followed by a 'padded pudding with mock cream', another one of Marguerite Patten's recipes, which now were slightly improving.

The girls, like many, made the best of the time and managed to have some fun; as they all agreed, goodness knows what sort of Christmas their men were having. Later that evening, they joined some other neighbours and sang Christmas carols and many war-time popular songs.

Early in the new year, Nellie received a letter from Tommy informing her that he was due some leave and because of the delay in post getting through, his leave was now imminent. Nellie was overflowing with excitement, she had left Mary's house just after Christmas as agreed and was now frantically cleaning and polishing their house in readiness. Nellie had been and checked on her elderly neighbour, Mrs Anderson, and her son to ensure that they were managing and did not require anything.

"Yes, we are fine, dear. I have to admit there were times when I thought that we were in danger of being bombed, but we seem to have missed the worst, especially compared to some areas. Let's thank God we have been so fortunate."

Nellie went on to tell Mrs Anderson about Tommy coming home soon and that she was sprucing herself and the house up. Mrs Anderson gave Nellie an old dress that was once her own from her younger days when she and her husband would go out to somewhere special for the evening.

"I know that it is a very old-fashioned style, my dear, but I am sure that a clever girl like you could make something from it and I would rather see it used than just lying up in the attic."

Nellie was ecstatic; the fabric was silk and lace and yes a bit old-fashioned, but once a few alterations were made, it would be a fabulous garment and very special.

Tommy arrived on the doorstep and Nellie ran out with open arms and tears, kissing and hugging one another.

"Can I catch my breath and come in then, Nellie, where we can have a proper cuddle, instead of a display out here in the street for all to see?"

"I am just so happy to have you home, I don't care who sees us," laughed Nellie.

After much love making, they finally sat down and spoke about what had been happening to them during their separation. Tommy did not say too much or certainly not in any detail of all the things that he had seen and Nellie felt that the young Tommy who she had married had changed a little and was more serious and grown up, but then she guessed that this was bound to happen with all the sights and responsibilities that he must now face.

"Christ!" said Tommy as they went for a walk around the area. "I hardly recognise the place. It did have some serious bombings, didn't it, but the main thing is that you, Connie and Mary are safe, but so very sad to hear about the loss of your grandparents."

Nellie impressed Tommy with her new-found cooking skills; it might not have been fancy foods, but she had learned, mainly from Mary, how to make the most out of what little they had and her make do and mend dress from Mrs Anderson's old dress turned out to be a really beautiful dress, which after wearing to welcome Tommy home was returned straight back into the wardrobe and would await another special occasion.

Far too quickly, Tommy once again had to leave Nellie and return to his duties.

"Keep yourself safe please, Tommy, I miss you so much. Every night, I see your face before me as I go to sleep, then again in the morning when I wake."

"I also dream of you, my love, and pray to God to keep you safe from harm. One day, this will all be over and we can start to live our lives again."

Nellie went back into despair for a short time, but as before she kept herself busy with washing and cleaning her house until it was spotless. Mrs Anderson would often get Nellie to run some errands for her as she was now unable to go out herself and although her son was a great help to her sometimes, the queuing and waiting in the shops with the ration books was not something that he endured very well.

Bombings and air raids continued, but not with the ferocity over London that had been before and going into the air raid shelter was now almost routine. Mrs Anderson still declined Nellie's offer of going into the shelter and Nellie had to agree that for an elderly person to be in a damp cold shelter rather than her own warm bed was not an attractive alternative.

"As I said before, Nellie, I would rather die in my own warm bed than out there in the cold. I have to go sometime and I am getting rather tired now, so if that's the way God wishes me to go, then so be it."

Life ticked on and the rationing began to bite more, but with all the posters that the government displayed to encourage the nation to pull together with the war effort, everyone just got on with it and tried to help one another. Nellie visited Mary and Connie as much as she could and they would often come to her. Connie was still working at the Lyons tea house (she never informed them of her marriage) and would often make the girls laugh with stories of things that had happened at work.

One occasion when Connie visited Nellie, she just burst into tears.

"Whatever is wrong?" asked a concerned Nellie. "Nothing has happened to Pete, has it?"

"No, he is all right as far as I know. It is me, I'm pregnant."

Weeks turned into months and Connie was now starting to show a nice little bump. "Everything is going along fine, I have had my check up and the baby is growing nicely. I had to let work know that I was married and now obviously pregnant, they were not pleased as you can imagine, but I can stay and see the last of the month out."

"What will you do then, you know that you can come and stay here with me," suggested Nellie.

"Thank you so much but Mary has already offered to help support me and continue living with her. I do not know what we would do if we did not have Mary in our lives. I have had a letter back from Pete and he is over the moon that he is going to be a dad and he can't wait to see me again and he said he will still love me even though I will be fat."

"Well, you just tell him that he is responsible for your 'fat'."

Nellie was so pleased for Connie and had started knitting baby things, but she felt a slight pang of jealousy, as she and Tommy had not been careful during their love making yet there was no baby for her.

One night, Nellie had a very restless night and could not settle, she also had some nightmares about her Tommy. In the morning, she could still not shake off the unsettled feelings that she had.

"Get a grip on yourself, Nellie Brown," she scolded herself and kept busy with housework, also checking on Mrs Anderson next door.

Later that afternoon, she decided that she would visit Mary again as she needed to focus on something else and shake off this troublesome feeling. As Nellie went to the front door, she was aware that there was someone coming up the pathway. Instantly she felt sick and as the doorbell rang she debated running to the back door and out of the house. Shaking with fear, she opened the door to her worst fears; there on the doorstep was someone holding a brown envelope, a telegram.

"He may not be dead, Nellie, it just says missing presumed dead," soothed Connie.

"No, he is dead. I know it because I can no longer feel him with me."

Nellie had not shed a single tear since she had received the telegram.

"I am really worried about her." Both Mary and Connie felt the same. They wanted Nellie to move back to Bethnal Green with them but Nellie was absolute in her refusal and there was no budging from her decision.

"I am staying over for a couple of days and no arguments, I have brought us a few things including a stew that Mary has kindly made for us along with a bottle of gin, so sit yourself down while I go and put the kettle on."

"Oh Connie, it is lovely to see you but you do not need to stay, I am perfectly fine on my own."

But one look at Nellie with her dark-rimmed eyes, lack lustre hair and loss of weight said otherwise.

"Well, I am here now, so sit yourself down while I go and put the kettle on, I am gasping."

Just as they had finished their tea so the sirens began to start up their wailing. Once again, things were gathered up and the girls ran out to the Anderson shelter. Nellie had made a couple of cushions to go on the wooden seat as it made it slightly less uncomfortable if the raids lasted any length of time and as always a flask of tea.

"The bombing sounds a bit further away at the moment," said Nellie, as the pair sat close together for warmth. Although they had blankets, the shelters were only made of metal, so they were not built for comfort.

"Do the family from next door still come in to shelter?" asked Connie.

"No, the children have been evacuated to Wales, I believe, and I think the mother has gone to her sister or something, I never really saw much of them."

"Oh bugger," cried Connie, "I have drank too much tea, I am busting for a pee."

"Well, you will have to use that metal bucket at the end there," replied Nellie as she pointed to where the bucket was.

"Bloody hell, you really did need to pee, it sounds like a waterfall in here."

At this, both girls started to laugh, then as Connie finished her pee, because they were laughing so much she then let out a loud fart.

"And finished with a full stop," said Nellie as tears started to fall from laughing, which then changed to the tears that she had held back for so long.

"I have been thinking," Nellie commented on one of her visits to the girls, "it has been a while now since I last heard about Tommy, so I have decided that it is now time for me to do my bit and you are now looking at a Land Army girl."

"Is that really what you want to do?" both women asked almost in unison.

"I have to accept that Tommy has gone and that I need to move on. I can no longer be a housewife and I need to do something useful for my country as our menfolk are."

"Well, good on you, girl. You realise it will be hard work especially in the winter?"

"I realise that, but I am young, strong and above all else I need to be occupied and fill my days."

"You certainly will be doing that all right. We are both really proud of you, Nellie, and it will be the making of you."

Plans were made and finalised. Connie had agreed to live in Nellie's house, as Nellie did not want the landlord to rent it to someone else. Also although Mary had not said anything, both girls suspected that she had a new man in her life, so by Connie moving out Mary had the privacy to entertain. Life for the three women was changing as each was moving into new territory.

Both Mary and Connie accompanied Nellie up to London where she would catch her train to Norfolk, which was where she had been assigned to.

"Oh, it is really happening, so much change for all of us, you will not be with me at the birth of my baby." Connie shed a few tears. "Will things ever be the same again?"

"Give over, Connie, I am not leaving the country. I will get back to see you both as often as I can and you will have Mary to hold your hand when you are in labour. I need to do this and in a funny way, I am looking forward to mucking out the animals in the wet, muddy fields."

The three women laughed at the thought as Nellie boarded the train then disappeared from sight.

Chapter 7

The train arrived at Norwich Station on time and Nellie had been informed that she would be met by a Mr Hogg the farmer on whose land she would be working on and that he would be waiting outside. Sure enough, there was a horse and cart waiting with a gentleman sitting on top smoking away.

"Hello, are you Mr Hogg?" enquired Nellie.

"Sure am, gel, I take it you are Miss Brown then? You have come at just the right time, it is now coming up to a very busy period on the farm and with the men away, we need all the help that we can get. I was very much against having females to replace the men as I don't think that they can manage as well, but if you are as useful as the other girls, then it won't be so bad."

"Nice to meet you too, Mr Hogg, my name is Nellie."

"Yep, I knows that, gel, that's what the paperwork said."

This is an interesting start, thought Nellie to herself.

"Did I hear you say that there were other girls working on the farm already, Mr Hogg?"

"There's two others and with you that makes three."

"Really," replied Nellie, but thought it wise to say it softly to herself.

The rest of the journey was spent in silence, but as the horse pulled the cart along, Nellie breathed in the clean fresh air, no smell of burning buildings, or any dust particles floating in the air. Everywhere looked green, clean and fresh. Nellie closed her eyes and listened to the different bird sounds, the rhythmic sound of the horse's hooves clicking on the roadway as he trotted along was causing her to feel relaxed and sleepy, picking up on the various scents lingering on the air, some more pleasant than others. Nellie felt that she would enjoy being in the countryside and it may be just what she needed.

"Good afternoon to you. Nellie, is it?" asked the farmer's wife. She was a small round-shaped women but had a jolly friendly face. She wore an apron over her ample chest and well-worn clothes but everything in the kitchen was spotless, so she obviously kept a well-run house.

"Sit down, me dear, I'll make us a cup of tea, I bet you could do with one after your long journey. The other girls are still out working on the farm, young ones they are like you. I am sure that you will all get along fine. I do hope so anyway as you are all in the one bedroom. My three lads are all away fighting; two are in the army and my eldest Johnny is in the air force. We do have quite a few air basis around these parts, you know."

Nellie took an instant liking to this lady and felt that with all her chatter, she was probably glad to have some female company for a change.

"Now we have had our tea, I will show you to your room. It is very basic, I am afraid, but it is home to me and my family. By the way, my name is Jenny, it is really Jennifer but everyone 'round these parts calls me Jenny and my husband's name is Bernard. I don't suppose that he introduced himself, did he? Right, here you are then, lass, I will leave you to get settled and maybe try your uniform on if you haven't already. If it needs any alteration, just bring it down to me to fix. Oops, I should say that the bed over there nearest to the window is Samantha's and the one on the left is Jo's so this one here is yours."

The room was very basic and cold, there was a small window to the front which, when Nellie looked out of, had wonderful views over the green fields where sheep and cattle grazed. Who would even know that there was a war on, thought Nellie.

The other occupants had a few of their possessions on dilapidated chairs next to their beds. There was a stand in the remaining small area in the room where a wash jug and basin stood, some folded towels next to the basin looked clean but certainly not new.

"Obviously that must be for us to wash in, I thought that my house back in London was basic, but still I am not here as a holiday but to work."

As Nellie looked back out of the window and took in the scene again, she breathed in the fresh air, warmed by the summer sun and thought how much her Tommy would have loved the peace and tranquillity. Then, reflecting back over the short time that they had shared together and the things that they had planned to do, the tears started to sting her eyes.

"Oh Tommy, why did you have to join up so early and why did you have to leave me so soon?"

"Everything all right up there?" came the sound of the farmer's wife. "Everyone will be back in a few moments and I shall be serving up dinner."

Mr Hogg and the two girls returned back home.

"Something smells delicious, Jenny, as always," one of the girls commented as she washed her hands in the scullery.

Brief introductions were made. "Do you mind if we have a proper chat after dinner?" asked one of the girls who Nellie now knew was Samantha. " I am bloody ravenous."

The girls all helped Jenny with the clearing away. They were not expected to do the household chores, but there was a fondness for this friendly lady that they chose to help out. Washing, drying and everything cleared away, cups of tea were made and everyone sat down in the lounge, which was not a very big room; it just had a sofa and two battered-looking armchairs which were placed either side of the fire along with a Welsh dresser displaying all the china. It did not leave too much room for anything else, but with the fire lit and a couple of small lamps on, it was a very cosy area.

"So, Nellie, have you worked anywhere else as a Land Girl or is this your first time away from home?" asked Samantha. "By the way, I prefer to be called Sam."

"Yes, this is my first time away from London and it is all so very different. Out here, you would not know that we were at war with the Germans. It all seems so quiet and peaceful."

"You will when you hear the aircraft going over. You see, here we have quite a few airfields, some are large bases especially the yanks, but some small aircraft are able to land in farmer's fields, but it can be good fun as we are sometimes invited to dances at the nearby basis or local village halls."

"Remember, girls, that we do have a curfew which you are expected to respect, else you will be moved to another area where perhaps there is not as much fun to be had. You are paid to work not gallivant around."

"Stop nagging, Bernard, the girls so far have respected the curfew and they do need to have some fun in these awful times; after all, they are still young," replied Jenny.

Nellie was starting to feel sleepy. After such a wonderful meal of meat potatoes and vegetables (not such harsh restrictions as in the city as much of the food would be grown on the farms), Nellie was starting to feel more relaxed and felt that the dynamics of the environment was positive.

"Well, we had best be getting off to our beds as it is up early again in the morning. Do you want us to milk the cows first thing or are you doing it, Mr Hogg?"

"I reckon that Jenny can teach Nellie how to do the milking, Jo can see to the chickens and if you deal with the pigs, after that the three of you can give me a hand in the fields."

"Right, then, see you all in the morning bright and early."

"I was worried there," said Nellie, "for a minute I thought that I was going to be thrown in at the deep end and be expected to milk a cow without being shown."

"No, Bernard is pretty fair, but be warned, he expects that after you have been shown once how to do something then that is it, he will not show you again. It was a bugger trying to learn how to manoeuvre that old rust bucket of a tractor out there," laughed Jo, "but if you get stuck, just give one of us a shout. After all, we are here to help one another as well as the war effort. If you don't mind me asking you, Nellie, are you OK? Only at dinner time, it looked as if you had been crying. We won't interfere with your private life unless you wish to share but remember, we do try and give each other support when it is needed and Jenny is like a mother hen and she will always listen. We both felt very lonely and homesick when we first arrived but you will soon settle down and life here is not so bad, especially when you hear how some of the other girls have to live and describe their lodgings."

Nellie awoke the next morning to the most enticing smell she had not experienced for a long time.

"Is that eggs and bacon I can smell?"

"We need a good start to the day, as the work is hard and the day is long in the summer," replied Jenny.

After a short period of time, the girls began to form a close bond and relied on one another for emotional support as well as the physical. Work on the farm could be very hard; the girls were expected to do the same work as the men had previously carried out. They milked the cows, which Nellie actually enjoyed doing once she got the hang of it. She felt the warmth of the animal against her body and it felt quite comforting, unless the cow was not in a co-operative mood, then it was a different matter. Collecting the chickens eggs from out of their coop, then go into the field and help scythe the hay in readiness for hay making, so many chores to be done each day that as a city girl Nellie had never given any thought to.

The girls wore standard uniforms of brown corduroy breeches, brown brogues, fawn knee-length woollen socks, a green V-necked pullover, a fawn shirt and a brown cowboy style hat. The girls would often adapt their uniforms to suit themselves especially in the summer when their breeches often became shorts. Often the girls wore scarves over their heads, tied at the top, to prevent their long locks getting in the way and worse getting caught in any machinery.

Nellie liked both girls equally; Sam was a very attractive woman of 24 years the same age as Nellie, but there the similarities ended. Sam had been brought up in a large house in London; her father was a very wealthy business man. Sam had led a privileged life of plenty with a private education, in comparison to Nellie and Jo, but although she spoke very 'plummy', she was also a bit dippy and not very worldly wise at times, Sam was also what Nellie would describe as a solid-built girl, certainly not ballerina material. She had been used to horse riding and other outdoor pursuits, she was a physically strong woman.

"With your upbringing and lifestyle, what are you doing here working as a Land Girl?" asked Nellie, realising as she said it that it might have been a little impertinent to ask.

"Well, Mummy and Daddy had four girls of which I am the youngest. My sisters were all very 'girlie' and loved pretty clothes and very feminine pursuits, they have all married well and have beautiful homes and children. I was never like them, I loved horse riding and walking and certainly did not enjoy dressing up as a demure-looking female. I mean look at me, my build alone does not lend itself to being delicate and dainty. I am more like a bloody cart horse, so working on the land is far more up my street. Also if the young Princess Elizabeth with all her family's money can do her bit for the country, then so can I. If I am honest, I think that my parents believed that after a month or so, I would return home and give up on my war effort, but as you can see, I do not look like a typical debutante and the type that enjoys all the refinement of fancy dresses and balls. I am far more down to earth and happier mucking out and riding my horses across open fields and having the odd fall in the mud, so with some persuasion, here I am. So you have to forgive my voice but truly I do not wish to be any different to you two and secretly I much prefer to live on a farm than in the large house I was brought up in. I can get dirty, fart like a horse, smoke and swear without anyone tut-tutting behind me."

Nellie and Jo roared with laughter at Sam's easy and honest way. Nellie started to really warm to Sam and hoped that the future could once again be filled with fun and laughter.

"How about you, Jo, what made you join?"

Jo was a slim, petite young woman. She had unruly mousey-coloured hair which curled to however it wished and would not be tamed by a brush or comb, but it framed her small face beautifully and although Jo appeared to the eye to be of a delicate nature, she was like a lion with a strength of mind and will that outdid the other two.

"I have three brothers who are older than me and they have left home to fight. I did not wish to be at home and not doing my bit, so although my mum wanted to me to stay at home with them both, she could understand I needed to spread my wings and do something useful and as I am now 22 years old, with most of the fit men gone off to fight what was the point of staying at home and waiting for romance to come?"

"So, now it is your turn, Nellie, what has brought you here?"

Nellie went on to tell the girls of her reasons for joining up and leaving London. She surprised herself that since she had started to release her inner emotions, although a very long way from recovered, she was at least able to tell the girls some of her story.

"Well," said Jo, "as we said before if you want to talk, we are here for you but if you wish to be alone, then we will respect that as well."

They all wished one another a good night, and within minutes, Nellie realised that both of the girls were sound asleep, so she put her face in the pillow and allowed the tears to come again as she cried herself to sleep.

Morning was heralded by the sound of the rooster making everyone aware of his presence, then before Nellie had even opened her eyes, she felt the early morning sun on part of her face as it attempted to make its way into the room via the small window. Birds were singing determined not to be outdone by the rooster. The cacophony of birdsong close by made her smile and for the first time in a long while, she felt alive again and was determined that no matter how hard she was expected to work, she would try to embrace and enjoy this new chapter in her life.

Chapter 8

"Have you ever driven a tractor before, Nellie?" asked Mr Hogg, or as he now allowed the girls to call him, Bernard.

"Don't get too many opportunities in the part of London where I lived," replied Nellie with a cheeky grin on her face.

Despite his reservations, Bernard was warming to the three girls; each had their own qualities and had very different characters, but they worked well together as a team and even he had to admit they were hard workers. Bernard knew of some of the other farmers that took most of the Land girls' wages which were set by the government and claimed that it was for 'expenses' board, lodgings and food, but he was a very fair man and believed that if you treated someone fairly, you would get it back and he felt that the girls worked hard, never moaned and were good to his wife and gave her some female company, so all in all, he felt that it had all worked out well.

"Mind you," he muttered to himself, "it would not be good to let them see me softer side too often." It keeps them on their toes, he reckoned.

"Right then, let's get started on teaching you how to drive. It will be harvesting time soon and I need to rely on all of you to be able to use the farm machinery safely. The three of you also need to understand some of the terminology, so that if anyone calls out for something, you will know what they mean."

"You're a natural," said Jo as she watched Nellie manoeuvre the tractor around the farm.

Nellie gradually got used to turning the handle to start the tractor which was situated at the front of the machine; it took a while but once mastered, it became easier. Also learning to let the clutch up slowly so that the tractor moved away at a steady pace was essential, because the men and women would need to pitch the sheaves of corn on to the wagons where they were stacked by a man called the 'loader'.

"So now all you girls have been trained to use a tractor safely and have some understanding of the various commands, come autumn when it is harvest time, it will be all hands to the pump. It is a very busy time in the farming calendar."

As always, Bernard spoke gruffly to the girls, but they were all starting to like the character more as they saw through his rough exterior and understood that deep down, he was quite a softy, but he had a tough job to do and expected it to be carried out.

Nellie began to settle down and surprised herself with what jobs she could actually perform well and that she enjoyed the life she was now living. The farm itself was quite basic but it was always warm and with hot food and drink waiting at the end of the day, it was very homely. It was a mixed farm of arable land and dairy, with beef cattle, sheep, pigs and poultry and the girls were gradually learning how to cope with them all.

The farmhouse consisted of quite a reasonable-sized kitchen where there was a range stove that was fuelled by logs stored outside under a covered way, which kept the kitchen area constantly warm. Jenny was an excellent cook and everyone looked forward to the mealtimes. The small sitting room as described earlier was just off the kitchen, so the warmth from the kitchen and with the fire lit on an evening if required was wonderful, compared to upstairs, which often felt cold as apart from the rising heat had no other form of heating. Toilet facilities were in a small shed at the end of the garden consisting of a wooden plank with a hole cut in and a bucket underneath. Toilet paper consisted of old newspaper cut into squares hanging from a meat hook. Jenny had the unsavoury job of emptying the bucket into a larger tank further down the garden and once a week the 'slop man' would come and empty all the neighbouring tanks in his horse and cart and take the unsavoury liquid away. Bath time consisted of a tin bath once a week which was placed in front of the fire and the water heated in the old copper kept in the scullery. The girls were very lucky, because not too far from the farm, there was a large house belonging to some local gentry who gave permission for the girls to have a 'shallow bath' once a week at their house in the servants quarters. Although it was a good mile to walk to get to the house, the girls enjoyed the privacy it provided much more.

"Who actually lives in that big house?" asked Nellie one day after being shown where it was located.

"That is where General Barrett and his wife live. He is the landowner of most of the farms in this area. Sometimes, you may see them down in the village, they oversee many of the things that go on here in these parts. When the evacuees are sent here, Mrs Barrett allocates them to various homes. Some poor sods are then used as servants and are poorly treated and become very homesick and miserable. I have sometimes seen them outside a house sobbing, it breaks my heart to see them so distressed but I suppose their families feel that they are safer here than with the bombing, but I do wonder how it will affect them mentally. Others are luckier and have a very happy time, they are well-treated and in some cases well-loved. Compared to their lives in London, it must feel like paradise. At Christmas time, apparently Mr and Mrs Barrett hold parties for the locals in their house and the children are all given small gifts, so by all accounts they are pretty good people, although one of their sons has not got such a good reputation, but he is serving his country at the moment.

"Right, we had best get back and get them cows milked," suggested Sam.

Nellie was woken early the next morning by such a commotion from outside. As she wiped the sleep from her eyes and gathered her thoughts, she jumped out of bed and looked through the window to see what the noise was all about. Nellie had to smile to herself; outside the pigs had escaped their pen and were not going back willingly and without a fight. There was the farmer and his wife, desperately trying to catch them or corner them to no avail. Nellie pulled up her trousers and threw on a jumper and with her Wellington boots on went to give a hand, shortly followed by the others. They all attempted to catch the evasive pigs. Nellie at one time thought that she had a firm hold on one, only to lose control, ending up sliding into the wet soil from the overnight rain. As she got up, her body and face were covered in mud and now with wet hands trying to get hold of the slippery creatures was even harder. Eventually, after what seemed like hours, the escaped pigs were now back in the pen and the hole that the escapees had fled from was repaired, five weary, hungry and thirsty souls returned to the farm house for some well-earned breakfast.

Once breakfast was speedily over, the cows started to create a noise. It was now past milking time and they were letting everyone know it, and so another day had begun.

Time seemed to go by quickly and thankfully for Nellie, because there was so much to do each day she did not have so much time to dwell on her private thoughts. At night, as she drifted off to sleep, she always said a goodnight to her Tommy, Connie and Mary. Nellie had written to Connie and given her the address of where she was staying and of her life in the country. She asked how her pregnancy was going and generally how things were in London, but was still waiting for a reply.

"There's a letter for you," said Jenny as she handed it to Nellie one day.

"It's from my friends in London," she called out as she made her way back upstairs to read in private.

Everything was pretty much as it was when she had left; bombs continued to rain down over various parts of London with more loss of life and buildings. Connie stated that she was as big as one of the barrage balloons that was flying overhead, but otherwise it would seem that both her and the baby were doing well. Connie's suspicions of a romance between Mary and a gentleman had proved to be correct, so she tended to stay at Nellie's house more and more, giving the couple some privacy. It would appear that he was a serving officer in the air force, single and from a wealthy family. By all accounts, he treated Mary well and she appeared to be very happy. Connie promised to keep Nellie up-to-date with events as best she could and said that they were missing her, but were really delighted that she was enjoying her new life.

Harvest time was now upon them and as Bernard predicted, it was very busy on the farm. Farmers from around came to help as it appeared that this was how it worked in the farming community, moving from one farm to another as each helped the other with the work load. Farm hands that had not gone off to fight for whatever reason, young boys and reservists were called upon to help. Also if there were any Italian POWs stationed nearby, it was every pair of hands to help with the job of cutting, gathering and stacking the hay.

Nellie, one evening, although absolutely shattered, went outside into the field and looked out where once there was a flowing field of corn now stood a field of neatly shaped hay stacks which, in the moonlight, looked almost magical. The silence of the night was only disturbed by the owls hooting along with the distant bark of a dog, bats could be seen flying around probably making the most of insects being disturbed by the cutting down of the corn. Nellie smelt the air which seemed to carry a very pleasant scent of the new-mown hay. Life on the farm was definitely not an easy one but right at this moment certainly beat the life in London that she had left behind.

Standing alone in the darkness, she felt a calmness come over her, like someone had just wrapped a warm blanket around her shoulders and given her an embrace.

No matter what happens to us in life, the cycle will continue, she thought as she made her way back inside.

"Now for the time of celebrations, it is the Harvest Festival," said Jenny. "We hold a party in the local village hall where everyone joins in and brings produce and homemade wines and beers and we generally have a grand old time. Those that have musical instruments bring them along, a piano is often made use of as well. Consequently, not much work other than the essentials is carried out the next day. This is a great reward for all the hard work carried out by everyone during the season and they can let their hair down. Mind you, it is a good job that the hall is within easy walking distance, so we can at least stagger home again."

The girls laughed at this and became excited at the thought of a party.

"What shall we wear for the dance tomorrow night?" enquired Nellie. "It is so long since I have been out, I am not sure if I have anything suitable."

"Here, let's have a look at what we have between us and see if we can't manage to pull something out of the bag," suggested Sam and Jo.

Between the girls and with Nellie's skills at the sewing machine, they made some lovely dresses out of previous old-fashioned outfits.

"You're pretty good at this make do and mend lark, Nellie, you have made us all look very presentable. Now who has any eye liner and we can put a seam line in our legs."

Because the girls rolled up their shorts during the summer months whilst they worked in the fields, they all had bronzed legs, so with the pencil line added it really did look as though they wore stockings.

It turned out to be a great night with lots of music, singing and dancing, but the most surprising thing of all was young Jo. After drinking a glass or two of homemade elderflower wine, she got up onto the small stage that had been erected for the 'band' and she sang like a bird.

"Where has that voice come from?" exclaimed Bernard. "She's such as slip of a thing and here she is belting out some songs' mind you, she is also a strong lass for her size as well."

"Is that a compliment you are giving out there, Bernard?" said Nellie with a smile on her lips. "Well, that's a first."

Bernard had been caught out, his softer side had slipped through after a few beers.

"Can a man not say something good without having the mickey taken?" he grumbled and strode off to resume his beer with his fellow farmers.

Nights were drawing in now and so was the cold.

"It's freezing up here in this room," moaned young Jo.

The other two suspected that Jo was starting to feel homesick lately as the usually happy Jo was now more morose and grumpy.

"When are you due some time off, why don't you go home and see your family?"

"I know that my mum misses me and often asks in her letters when I will be returning home."

"Well then, ask Mr Hogg, if you can be spared for a time. After all, the busiest period is now over."

Christmas was just around the corner, Jo had been given some home leave, so the workload increased slightly for the other two, but they managed and they were both glad for Jo.

Mary had written to Nellie informing her that after a difficult birth, Connie now had a baby boy and that they were both doing well. Pete had managed to be home on a short leave of only two days, but at least he got to see his son. Everyone there was well despite the bombing raids, although said Mary they were fewer than earlier in the year, they were still using the underground as a shelter when the sirens went off and that they now had it worked out perfectly especially with young 'Billy', the new arrival. She went on to say that rationing was getting tougher and the queues outside the shops were getting longer and with no guarantee that there would be anything left when your turn came, but with the British spirit they endured, as they say "what doesn't kill you makes you stronger".

Mary ended her letter with sending their love and hoped to see her soon and to take care of herself. Nellie tried hard, but she felt that although Mary had kept the letter light, there was hardship and struggle back in London and she wept for them.

Nellie decided that when Jo returned, she would ask to be allowed some leave to go and see her friends.

Holly and Ivy with paper chains were put up in the small room. Although paper had to be saved and not wasted, they all felt that a few chains would not be too wasteful. Twigs that had fallen were twisted into small wreaths with a few winter berries to decorate, making the room feel more festive. Nellie had been secretly making small gifts for the ladies. During the season, she had managed to find some lavender that was growing in a field nearby when she was out walking one day. How it had got there she did not know, but she picked the small bunches when they were dry, hid them until the flowers fell off the stems and put them into a small container until ready to use. From an old blouse of hers that had been worn until the seams were coming apart and the fabric so thin it was shredding in places, Nellie sewed the fabric into circles in which she placed a few pieces of lavender, tied up with a piece of string, it made little fragrant linen bags.

Christmas on the farm was very good. They were able to have chicken with roast potatoes and a few peas and carrots. What a luxury it was, especially as in the cities this would not have been possible, but because some of the produce could be grown on the farm, they made the most of it.

In the period between Christmas and the New year, whilst the girls were out clearing the ditches of the year's growth of foliage, a couple of large planes flew over quite low and very noisy.

"Bloody hell," said Nellie, "they scared the life out of me, look at the size of them."

Young Billy, a local lad of 13 years who was giving a hand on the farm, excitedly exclaimed that they were spitfires and hurricanes, planes that were probably from the nearby air base.

"Wow, they certainly are loud and intimidating, the noise of them going over gave me the shivers, bringing back the memories of the Blitz in London. God help the poor sods when that thing drops its bombs. I know that this is war, but all those innocent people like us who did not want a war are getting killed."

Thoughts then turned to Connie and Mary. *I must make the time and effort to go and see how they are doing but there is a part of me that is scared to return and see what has been happening since my absence. My life here is now so very different and as hard as it is up early and bed late, especially now in the winter when the days are shorter and so dark. I am afraid to go back into my past and the painful memories.* Nellie rubbed her cold hands together and resumed her work.

"Good news, girls, we have all been invited to a New Year's Eve party at the village hall and I have been informed that some airmen from the local American base have also been asked if they would like to attend."

"Hooray!" squealed Jo. "No offence, but there will be other men who are not farmers and will be of our own age to talk to."

"Farmers are not so bad," replied Sam. "Everyone had their suspicions that Sam was sweet on a local farmer who was a widower; she would always deny it, of course."

The hall was packed with people and yes there were a good few young American men there who were teaching the young ladies how to jitterbug and many got up to dance to the music. The Americans had cigarettes to hand around and to some lucky girls they even gave stockings.

"Real stockings," cried young Jo, "can you believe it?"

Jo was encouraged to get up and sing again. Now she had shown what she was capable of, she would regularly be called upon to use her talents and entertain everyone, and for this she was also given some stockings. Towards the later part of the evening, the band played some music by 'Glen Miller', an American band, and many young girls were invited up to dance.

"Hello, gorgeous, would you care to dance?" these words were spoken softly into Nellie's ears from behind. Her heart gave a lurch and she felt a shudder as she was reminded of the same words spoken by her Tommy a lifetime ago. Nellie turned and saw a young man who she had to admit to herself was good looking. His eyes were soft and gentle-looking as he gave her a sweet smile. He was not like some of the others she had been watching that seemed brash and very confident; this young man appeared to be more shy and quite in nature. Nellie did not know how to respond; should she dance, but then decided what harm could it do. After all, he was only asking for a dance.

For the rest of the evening, Nellie and Michael danced together and the conversation between them was easy and comfortable. Nellie felt that she had known him for years and he was such a comfortable person to be with. Michael told her that he was married and his wife was back home in America and Nellie spoke about her marriage and loss of Tommy. By the end of the evening, they talked like old friends. At the stroke of midnight when the clock chimed to herald in the New Year, it felt perfectly natural to kiss one another.

After all, it is only one friend kissing another, Nellie told herself.

Chapter 9

Winter was now gradually turning to spring and the start of new life around the farm was showing in the fields, hedgerows and also with the animals. Nellie had found the long cold winter evenings hard at times and it somehow made her feel lonely, although she had made good friends with the farmer's wife and fellow Land girls, she did often miss her old friends in London.

"Shake yourself out of it, girl," she told herself. "Compared to others, you have it pretty good under the circumstances."

Along with the other women during the winter months, they had knitted scarves and gloves for the men out fighting as so many other women had been doing, anything to help and make the men feel that they were constantly remembered by those back home. Nellie struggled at times with the knitting needles and gave up on the more complicated art of glove and sock making so she stuck with plain scarves and as for Sam, well, there were more knots and holes in her knitting than anything that remotely looked like knitting.

"I thought I was bad," exclaimed Nellie, "but your attempt at knitting looks more like a lace shawl!" Nellie then had to laugh as the knitting flew across the room straight at her.

"That, amongst many other crafting activities my mother never taught me, and to darn a sock or sew on buttons, well, that is just a mystery to me," moaned Sam, who really did want to try and do her bit.

"We have to accept, my dear, that there are tasks better suited to us than others," said Jenny. "I am sure that we can find you something else to do for the war effort."

Getting up early one morning as the sun was just peeking out from behind the horizon, Nellie noticed movement in the field. As she strained her eyes to focus in the half-light, there in the field were two hares chasing one another. She watched them for a while until they suddenly shot off at speed and disappeared from sight.

"It certainly is that time of year again where male thoughts are starting to focus on one thing, lucky buggers," she laughed to herself.

Splashing her face with cold water, she dressed ready to go downstairs as the other two stirred.

"Another day," said Nellie, "rise and shine, girls, there's work to be done."

Nellie by this time was mostly enjoying life in the country, she loved to see the change in the seasons and although she had enjoyed doing a bit of gardening in a small way in her own garden, this was on a much bigger scale, as on the farm they also grew potatoes, carrots and many other vegetables, so even though it was war-time, unlike in the cities they were never short of vegetables. Reminders that there was a war going on was mainly from the air as the large planes would fly over, going out from local bases and crossing over to Germany where they would head for their targets. Aeroplanes from Germany tended to head for the bigger cities. London and a heavy raid on Coventry, which very nearly wiped them off the map all in revenge of the bombing of Munich, were but two of the targets with a huge loss of life in both. Nellie would often think of her friends and how they were coping back in London, but thankfully, the hard work on the land helped to keep her mind occupied most of the time.

Nellie had met up a few times with Michael and they were now becoming good friends, he would talk about his life back home and that he was married but there were no children as yet.

"Thank god," he said, "now is most certainly not the time to bring babies into the world, not with all the uncertainty that is going on right now."

Nellie told him about her Tommy and how much she missed him and of Connie and her baby. They found conversation so easy between them that no conversation appeared strained or restricted. Often Michael would take her and the other girls to dances that were going on at the base or just walk out with Nellie; they gave comfort to one another and eased the loneliness that they both felt.

Michael then had to leave as he was called to go on a mission and would be away for some time. Nellie wished him well and to be safe. Michael then for the first time since the New Year's party bent down to face her and then gave her a very gentle kiss on the lips.

After a month or so, Nellie started to miss his company and although continued to work hard on the farm, she began to have that lonely feeling again, so after getting permission to have some leave she went back to London to see Connie, Mary and baby Billy.

"It's so good to see you again," said Connie and Mary as hugs and kisses were given all 'round.

"Oh, I have missed you both so much. Where's the little man then?" asked Nellie.

"Sleeping at the moment so let's have a cuppa and catch up before he wakes."

The three women sat down and chatted and chatted for what seemed like hours. Nellie could not help noticing how pale and tired Connie looked and had also lost quite a bit of weight, but she chatted like the old times and they both commented on how well Nellie looked.

"You look so well, how is life out there on the farm in Norfolk? It certainly looks as if the fresh air suits you," said Mary with a happy smile on her face. Loud protesting noises came from upstairs. "His lordship awakens," laughed Connie as she got up from her chair and headed off to collect young Billy.

"Is everything all right with Connie?" asked a concerned Nellie. "She looks worn out."

"Things have been very difficult here lately, what with the rationing and the effects of the war in general, also her Pete was home on leave recently and they stayed in your house and from what Connie was saying, he appears to be a changed man. Apparently, he was aggressive to her and having bad nightmares most nights, waking up screaming. He would also not have much to do with the baby, especially when he was unsettled. I do believe that Connie felt it a huge strain, she feels that he is not the man she married. We do not have any idea of what life is like for these men, what they see, have to do and put up with and I am sure that when they come home, they want to have things as normal as possible, but it must have an effect on them mentally, so I hope that Connie can bear with him and hope that when all of this is over, things may go back to how they were but who knows."

Connie returned to the room with the most gorgeous baby Nellie had ever seen, he gave her a huge beaming smile that showed one tooth at the front.

"Oh Connie, he is adorable!" As she put out her hands to take him, Nellie was surprised at how heavy he felt. "Wow, are you giving him your share of rations as well, Connie? He is certainly a good size and weight."

Billy just gurgled away and was enjoying all the attention. Later that evening, when they had all retired for the night, Nellie could hear Connie's soft voice singing a lullaby, helping to settle Billy for the night.

I always knew that she would make a good mother. With a slight pain in her heart, Nellie slipped off to sleep.

Thankfully, that first night they had all been able to sleep soundly in their beds, but the following night, the air raid siren sounded and the well-practised mission of making their way down to the underground station was carried out.

"When will it all end?" cried Connie, who was usually strong and resilient gave way to her tears.

It was time for Nellie to return to Norfolk and resume her work on the farm. She was very concerned about Connie, but Mary had reassured her that she would keep an eye on them both and keep them safe and Nellie knew that this was true and that no harm would come to them while Mary was in charge.

Spring and summer were once again drawing to a close and all were getting ready for the harvest. Nellie worked now like she was born to it; she enjoyed the milking of the cows, looking after the hens and so forth. Ditch clearing and maintenance she was not as fond of, although she did enjoy driving the tractor. Having said that, Nellie was not so keen on attending to the pigs.

"That bloody pig has really taken a dislike to me, it runs to me every time I go into the pen. I have told it that it is the first in line for the chop and I will have great joy in eating it,"

"Perhaps it just loves you and runs to you as a greeting," commented Sam with a smile.

Harvest festival plans were in place as all the farmers had their hay safely in. Again it was hard work but as before, with everyone available and helping out, including the Italian POWs who sang while they worked most times, actually made it a little more enjoyable as the men certainly were able to sing.

During the festivities, Nellie noticed a familiar figure entering the barn. At first, she was slow to react but then she realised it was Michael so she ran towards him and gave him a big hug; although she desperately wanted to kiss him, sensing that he would have preferred that as well, but she decided that it might not be appropriate.

Michael and Nellie resumed their meetings and the friendship was starting to take on a new turn.

"Remember that you are married and have a wife back home waiting for you, Michael. We must not take this friendship to the next level as much as I would like to," said Nellie, although her heart was aching to be taken into his arms and him making love to her.

"It is so difficult," said Michael, his voice now low and husky. "I want you so much and although I know it would be a betrayal to my wife, I may also be killed on our next mission."

Although Nellie managed to persuade him that it would be wrong, she knew that it was only a matter of time.

Christmas was spent as the previous years, but with one missing; the suspected romance between Sam and the farmer living nearby had blossomed and Sam was spending Christmas day and Boxing day with him.

"So, we may hear the sound of wedding bells soon then," said Bernard, who never usually said much or involved himself in the women's lives, preferring to spend any free time that he managed to get with his fellow farming friends. "I wonder how her posh parents will take that news."

New Year's Eve party was to be held in the local village hall and there was to be a local band playing the now popular Glen Miller's music. Nellie invited Michael along. Sam came with her partner and by now, young Jo also had a man in her life who attended with her. Dancing and singing went on through the evening and everyone was up on the floor when it was time to ring in the New Year. Nellie and Michael embraced each other and the kiss this time was not just a friendly peck but a long, lingering, sensual kiss, that they both knew would take them further.

"I have taken the liberty of booking a room at the local hotel for the night if you are happy," said Michael, "but although I wish it with all my heart, I will understand if this is not what you want."

Nellie at that moment in time needed him and willingly went along with his request.

Initially, they were both nervous but once they started to kiss, it seemed to be the most natural thing in the world to happen and nothing else mattered. Nellie had a strong need to be in the arms of a man again and it felt good. They made love for most of the night, they even surprised themselves as to how much energy they had. Neither had any regrets in the morning as they parted to go their separate ways.

"Where were you last night?" laughed Sam and Jo, giving each other a sneaky wink that had not gone unnoticed by Nellie.

Nellie felt that her life was content again, although she knew that it could not last. Michael had a wife to return to after the war, but she decided that for the time being, she would enjoy what time she had with him and worry about the future when the future came. After all, she knew only too well how quick things could be taken away again.

A letter arrived shortly into the New Year and Nellie recognised Connie's writing. Anxious that it may be bad news, Nellie asked to be excused for a few minutes.

"Hope that this letter finds you well and that you had a good Christmas and New year. Did you get to see your American friend at all?" The letter continued with news of home and how things were, then the letter concluded with the bombshell that Nellie was going to be an auntie again.

"Bloody hell, Connie!" Nellie exclaimed out loud. "You don't half make life difficult for yourself," and she wondered how she would manage, but she supposed with the help of Mary she would. Nellie then sat for a few moments thinking how lucky she had been in being able to conceive a baby not just once but twice and for herself there was no such luck.

Nellie had never taken any precautions but accepted sadly that maybe she would be one of life's childless women.

"Come on 'girl', don't just sit here feeling sorry for yourself. There is work to be done."

Nellie continued to meet up with Michael whenever time permitted and they made love as often as they could. She kept telling herself that it would one day all end in tears and that he would return to his wife, but equally she enjoyed having the arms of a man around her again and the feeling of being wanted and needed was fulfilled.

"I will be going away soon, Nellie," said Michael. "I do not know for how long or where, not that I would be at liberty to say anyway, but I want you to wait for me because on my return, there is something I wish to say and discuss. Meanwhile, until my return I would like you to wear this ring on your finger and keep it safe please."

"Oh Michael, it is beautiful but I cannot accept it." The ring was gold and set in it was a large sapphire stone.

"Please, Nellie, I want you to wear it."

"Michael, it would be wrong. You are a married man and you must return to your wife after the war has ended."

"That is what I wish to discuss when I return. I love you Nellie, so let's not waste any more precious time now talking, that will be for later now let's enjoy our last moments together." Michael picked Nellie up in his arms and carried her off into the hay barn.

Nellie wore the ring as she promised she would, not on her wedding finger as she felt that would be wrong but on her right hand instead. The others all questioned her about it, but Nellie just replied that it was a friendship ring and nothing else.

Nellie felt like a young girl again and at times like walking on air then at others, she had the feeling of a dark cloud in the distance that was looming towards her.

Work continued on the farm. The ground had to be turned over after the winter frosts had broken it up in readiness for the planting of potatoes, by now the girls just got on with the work as they knew exactly what had to be done and when. They all enjoyed the work, although hard, the friendship between them was strong. Sam by now had got engaged to the farmer but until they were married, she would remain working on Bernard's farm.

"How did your parents take the news?" asked Nellie and Grace once they were engaged.

"I don't know, I have not told them yet," replied Sam, laughing. "It really does not matter. I am a grown woman now and make my own choices in this world, but I feel sure that when they meet Eddy, they will like him."

"Nellie, a telegram has just arrived for you," explained the breathless Jenny as she made her way across the muddy field.

Nellie took the telegram, anxious and her mind in a whirl; the last time she received one of these was to inform her about Tommy.

"Oh please, don't let it be Michael," she said to herself.

"Nellie, please come home, Mary involved in fatal accident. Love Connie."

Nellie went ashen-faced and passed out. When she recovered, she found herself on the sofa with Jenny at her side.

"Whatever has happened?" enquired the concerned women.

"I have to return to London," replied the tearful Nellie. "It appears that Mary who was like a mother to me has died in an accident, I don't know any more than that at the moment only that I must return. As far as I know," continued Nellie, "Connie and myself are the only living relatives that Mary has. I am sorry to just leave you so suddenly but I need to be with Connie right now." With this, Nellie ran up the stairs to pack what few belongings she had.

"I will leave my Land Army uniform here in the event that I may return," called out Nellie from upstairs.

Nellie was given compassionate leave, so after her hurried goodbyes, tears and the promise that they would all meet again, Nellie kissed Sam and Grace goodbye.

Bernard and Jenny took Nellie to the station, the friendship and bond between them had become so strong over the last two years that they treated the girls like their own.

Nellie had initially protested and said, "the farm is too busy for you to leave it and take me to the station," but the couple would not hear of it and before Nellie boarded the train, even the normally gruff Bernard gave her a kiss on the cheek.

"I will miss you all so much, but I will return some time to visit. Take care of yourselves, I will never forget you."

With a hiss of steam, the train then started to make its way out of the station.

During the journey back to London, Nellie's thoughts went to Michael. *I don't suppose we will ever meet again, you need to return to your wife as much as I would wish differently, it is the right and proper thing to do,* but she vowed that she would always wear the ring that he gave her.

Chapter 10

Arriving back into London, Nellie looked around her; the landscape was again changed from her previous visit. The remains of even more bombed buildings that had been badly hit or had sustained fire damage changed the landscape, areas that once had houses standing had been demolished for safety reasons and some looked to be in a very precarious state. Buildings where once families had lived and played out their daily lives were now no more than rubble, bricks and mortar. Some still had broken glass windows with the remnants of curtains blowing freely in the wind. Areas where once houses stood were now just empty spaces and any recognition of an area was difficult. Many of the buildings that had been damaged with windows and doors blown out but had remained structurally sound, people continued to live in; most often, more than one family shared the space because at least it was a roof over their heads keeping them dry.

Nellie noticed children wearing old shoes and clothes that were too big for them because their own clothes had been lost in the bombed out homes or they had grown out of their own shoes and now wearing an older sibling's or even their parents'. One lad apparently went to school in his mother's old high-heeled shoes, but in these times some footwear was preferable to nothing. Nellie was also struck by the smells, acrid in some cases, small flames could be seen, which probably resulted in a recent bomb attack were left to just burn out. Often people would wander over areas where presumably they once lived, looking for anything that maybe left in the rubble, old pictures or anything that was once a part of their life. Children, mostly boys, would also be searching for any 'treasure', shrapnel and the like would be collected, as for them it was more an adventure than heartache.

It appeared that although the people had lost so much, they continued to try and make the best of what they had and help one another. Friends and neighbours would give what little they could spare to another if their house had been bombed and were only left with what they were standing in. After all, the next bomb could have their name on it. Generally, there existed a community spirit of pulling together, helping one another in such awful times which was like a form of glue that would help to bond people together.

Mind you, thought Nellie, *not everyone has such a sense of community spirit, there are many that are only concerned about themselves.*

What a difference to how I have lived, it may have been very hard work and long days, but I have been better off than many of these poor souls in the heart of the bombing. Nausea was filling her senses as she neared Mary's house, another loss of a loved one had to be faced.

"Oh Nellie, am I glad to see you," cried Connie as she opened the door to Mary's house. Her eyes were red-rimmed and swollen from crying. Connie had decided to stay in the house for a short while until everything had been sorted out.

"What happened, how did Mary die? You said that it was in an accident, where is Mary now?" Nellie was tripping over her tongue as she asked so many questions.

Connie explained that Mary was buried within a couple of days and laid to rest in the nearby cemetery and that they would go the next day so that Nellie could say her goodbyes.

"What happened, was it a bombing raid?" questioned Nellie, anxious to understand how this tragedy had occurred, not giving Connie a moment's breath to explain.

"Take your coat off, sit down and catch your breath, Nellie. Billy is asleep upstairs so I will make us a cup of tea and tell you what happened."

"Apparently the air raid sirens went off and as usual people made their way to the underground, by all accounts the bombing had started causing a rush of people down the stairs at the same time. This caused a surge of people pushing, increasing the pressure on those at the front, so much so that by all accounts someone fell but the surge forward continued, causing others to also fall which resulted in people piling on top of one another crushing the people underneath them. Many died from crush injuries and asphyxiation, the details have been scant but unfortunately, our beloved Mary was one of them." Again, the girls began to cry and embrace one another.

"She was like a mother to us, how will we manage without her?" sobbed Connie. "It wasn't even a bomb that took her, just a tragic accident."

The girls sat for ages reminiscing and recounting stories that had happened in the house with Mary over the years, but mainly of how lucky they had been to have found her in their early days and how much they loved her.

"This bloody war!" exclaimed Nellie. "When will it ever end? So many lives lost and young men missing. Talking of which, how is your husband doing, have you heard from him?"

"He does not come home at all now," replied the tear-stained face of Connie. "The last time I saw him, he was a changed man, violent, drinking whatever he could get his hands on. It is sad but he is not the man I married. The war has changed him as probably it has many others, but I do not want him back if this is the man he has become. I know that probably sounds dreadful and very unsupportive, but with young Billy and this second one due in a couple of months, I am frightened that he may harm them or me."

"We have no idea of the horrors that our men have to face, no wonder so many have troubled minds and the difficulties they face when they return on leave," commented Nellie.

The two women talked and cried until the sounds of a child stirring from his slumbers reached their ears.

"That's the peacetime over with now that Billy is awake," said Connie attempting to smile. "I have my little one to think of now, what life have I brought him into." Connie wiped some tears from her face and then went upstairs to bring young Billy down. As they came down the stairs and into the room, Nellie was met with a beaming smile from an angelic-looking face.

"Oh Connie, what a gorgeous-looking baby he is."

"Don't be fooled by his smile, he can be a little monster when he wants to be, but I suppose most 18-month-old babies are the same."

Watching Billy interact with his mum and then playing with Nellie helped to lift the sad atmosphere and watching his antics made them both laugh.

"Oh," said Nellie, "he is an absolute joy to be around. He will help us both get through these dark days."

Once Billy had settled down for the night, the girls again sat and talked.

"Who paid for the funeral costs and everything?" asked Nellie. "I did not think that she had any close family."

"Mary had already made her own arrangements with the local undertaker at the beginning of the war, so that in the event of anything happening, we would not have to worry, but she only recently told me all of this; otherwise, I would not have known what to do, as I do not have that kind of money."

"Bless her, always thinking of others and not herself. We will miss her so much. What will happen to this house, will you stay here?" asked Nellie.

"I don't know what will happen, but Mary's solicitor has asked to see us both once you had returned from Norfolk."

"I wonder what that is about," said Nellie, as she started to make her way to the door. "I will say goodnight now, Connie. If you don't mind, I am shattered. Let's hope we have a quiet night without the sirens going off."

When Nellie went down to the kitchen in the morning, there was Billy sitting up in his high chair having his breakfast. As he saw her, he gave one of his huge toothy grins.

"Hey, that smile is enough to cheer you up in the morning, young man," said Nellie as she leaned over and gave him a big kiss, which he returned leaving a lovely smear of porridge on Nellie's cheek.

"I am sorry that I overslept but despite all the heartache, I actually had a good undisturbed night. How about you?" Nellie commented as she wiped the porridge from her face.

"Yes, I did too. Young Billy here just stirred for a short time but then went straight off again."

"Cup of tea?" asked Nellie as she moved to put the kettle on. As they sat drinking, Nellie asked what had happened to Mary's gentleman friend. "Only you never mentioned him yesterday, so I wondered if he knew or even if they were still together."

"Well, as you know Mary never really said much about him, only that they were just good friends and I haven't seen him for ages, so I am not sure what to do. Perhaps just wait and see if he turns up, but it would have been nice to let him know if we could."

"Maybe we will have to go through Mary's private things to see if there are any letters. Even though she has gone, it still does not seem right to poke through her private affairs, but if they were close, then we really should try and contact him."

After a few days of packing and crying, Mary's belongings were carefully folded and packed away with care. The girls had agreed that any clothing that fitted them they would keep, with rationing tightening and clothing shortages they both knew that Mary would be in full agreement that they kept the items and made use of them.

"She had some beautiful things," commented Connie, "too good to wear on a daily basis, but maybe in time to come when this war is over, we might have the opportunity to dress up and celebrate."

"Hopefully here is the information we need!" exclaimed Nellie as she opened a box containing letters.

They felt very uncomfortable opening Mary's personal mail and both just skimmed over the words.

"Here, this must be his name and address," as Connie lifted a letter that had not been posted.

Nellie and Connie agreed that they would write to this Mr D and hope that he was Mary's gentleman friend.

Friday of that same busy week, both girls went along to the appointed solicitor as requested. Billy fortunately was sound asleep in his pram so they were able to talk without disturbance. Both were very nervous, they had never had cause to speak to a solicitor before. Entering the solicitor's office of highly polished oak furniture and leather seats, the girls felt even more intimidated.

"I wonder why he wishes to see us," Connie whispered to Nellie as they saw the official-looking gentleman holding his hand out in greeting.

Surprised, excited and sad were the emotions that both Connie and Nellie felt as they left the imposing building.

"Who would have thought it, Mary kept that a total secret!" exclaimed Nellie.

Mary's will explained that in the event of her death, her property and all of her estate was to be sold and the money shared equally between Connie and Nellie, which amounted to quite a bit.

"Bloody hell, Nellie!" said Connie. "We are going to be rich!"

No return letter ever came from Mr D by the time the two women left Mary's property which they managed to sell fairly quickly.

"Oh well, we have left a forwarding address for him to contact us. It would be just devastating for him to arrive at the house and find strangers living there," commented Connie as she tucked young Billy into his pram.

Tearfully, Nellie and Connie walked from room to room of the now empty house, both remembered the first time they arrived and were welcomed by Mary. Nellie remembered bringing her grandmother to see where she would be living and working when she left them at the age of 19. In her mind's eye, there she was sitting with Mary, drinking tea. How excited the three girls were as they inspected and chose their rooms. Nothing more was ever heard of Grace who had left the house a couple of years earlier, presumably with the Canadian man she had spoken of.

Closing the front door and locking it, the girls then never looked back at the house again.

Chapter 11

Connie and her son Billy went with Nellie back to the house in Plaistow and they had decided that this was where they would live together until after the birth of the new baby, and possibly until the war had ended. Bombing over London and the East End had almost ceased for a while and it was hoped that it would all soon be over.

"Oh, it is good to be back home to my own place," said Nellie as she turned the key to her front door after being away so long.

Stepping back into the house, it felt like it had been a million years since her and Tommy had first arrived and he had carried her over the threshold.

"This damn war has changed ours and many others' lives so much, I think of the people that we have loved and lost in just a few short years, yet it feels like a lifetime. I understand that Mrs Anderson next door has passed away and that her son has since also moved out of the area, so she finally got her wish to be reunited with her husband, or that is how I like to see it. We shall have to wait and see who moves in next, I hope we are lucky and they are easy to get on with," Nellie commented.

"I believe that a new family are already in but I have not seen anyone yet, but when I have stayed here, I have heard some movement. Generally, I have flitted between here and Mary's, keeping an eye on the place and giving it an airing."

"Right then, gel," said Nellie, "no time for moping or reflecting too much as there is nothing to be gained, so let's put the kettle on and have a drink. We can then unpack our things before sorting out the sleeping arrangements."

The house did not take long to begin to feel more like home. There were only two bedrooms which were both of equal size. Nellie elected to have the front room so that she could look out and see what was going on outside, also just outside her front door on the pathway was a large cherry blossom tree that was well-established and Nellie remembered how beautiful it looked covered in pink blossom in the springtime. Sparrows would sit out on the branches and constantly chatter to one another, pigeons would strut around on the ground pecking at anything that might be food.

Although Nellie was glad to be back in familiar surroundings, she knew that she would miss the country side with all its smells and early morning bird songs.

"I do not think that I will miss the bloody cockerel waking me up at the crack of dawn," she muttered to herself, "although it would now be swapped by the sound of the milkman clanking down the road with the crates of milk rattling in his milk float."

Nellie would also miss the people that she had come to know along with the hard work that the Land girls carried out. But reflecting also on the fun that she had at the local dances and just fleetingly her thoughts went to Michael, wondering where he was now and how he was doing. Nellie had become very fond of him.

"Oh well, gel, that's the bloody war, our lives are like a cork on the sea at the moment, up and down and all over the place, nothing is settled." Nellie made a promise to herself that when the war was over, she would return to the farm to see everyone again, but for the time being the birth of the new baby was imminent so Nellie had no desire to leave Connie and Billy.

Connie by now was becoming very large and looking fit to burst.

"Blimey!" Connie exclaimed. "Nellie, there is only one in there, isn't there?"

"I don't remember my belly being so huge when I was expecting Billy," who by now was talking a few words and calling out for his 'Auntie Nellie' who was very fond of him and when his mummy could no longer bend over to pick him up, he had no problem getting cuddles from his Auntie Nellie. Rationing was still in force and getting tighter. There would be queues outside many shops and often by the time people got to the front, there was nothing left to buy. Making do and mending things came fairly easily to Nellie, although by now for many people, garments were worn almost to nothing and people would be seen with patches in their cloths, one clever lady was seen looking extremely smart in her thick fancy coat, but on closer inspection, it was actually made up from a candlewick bedspread. Many of the outfits that had been Mary's were being put to good use although some that the girls felt were too nice were saved for special occasions, not that there were too many of them. Some of the pieces that did not fit the girls were cut down and altered by Nellie, who possessed the ability to restructure garments. Many things were made into outfits for Billy, so nothing at all was wasted. Nellie also was able to make or adjust garments for the ever-increasing size of Connie.

Nellie began to clear some space around the Anderson shelter and grew a few vegetables in the small garden. They also managed to get hold of a couple of chickens which supplied them with a few eggs. This was great for Billy, as he would sit outside the coup for ages just watching and talking with these strange feathered friends. Nellie having worked on a farm tried to use some of the recipes that the farmer's wife had used, although in London they had less choice and availability than those in the country. Even so, with the help of Marguerite Patten and her war-time advice on food and nutrition, they managed.

One evening, as the girls sat and ate their food, Connie asked Nellie if she remembered some of the meals that she would put up for Tommy.

"Oh yes, especially that syrup pudding that ended up in the bin, what I would give to have that now," replied Nellie, laughing.

"Bugger, I think this is it!" Connie had woken Nellie in the night as she had started her labour pains.

"How frequent are the pains right now, Connie?" Nellie, ran to the phone box that was a few streets away and contacted the midwife who said that she would be there as soon as possible and asked Nellie to get everything ready for when she arrived.

The birth was a textbook one and Nellie marvelled at the way Connie seemed to take it all in her stride. "The whole street would know that I was in labour," laughed Nellie.

"Remember that this is my second baby and I know what to expect," replied Connie in between the contractions.

Young Billie's face the next morning when he awoke to a strange noise, then after going down the stairs was met with a stranger in the house that was making a dreadful noise.

"Good morning, Billy," came the voices of his mummy and Auntie Nellie. "Come and meet your baby sister."

It took Billy a while to come to terms with having to share cuddles and affection, but once he settled, he sometimes would help his mum with the baby and then other times he would totally ignore his baby sister and go and sit with his chickens. Life settled down and although Nellie felt that she needed to get out and work, she decided that Connie also needed some initial help of coping with two small ones.

Connie's husband never returned home again. Where he was or if even alive, she had no idea. Part of her was very sad as he would never know his daughter Elizabeth Mary.

"After the princess and our very dear friend," said Connie when she was deciding on a name. Connie was also fearful of him as on his last visit, he was violent and had taken to drink, but not knowing what had happened to the man she once loved filled her heart with some sadness.

"I presume that he has not been killed on active duty," said Connie one day. "Surely I would have been informed."

"So sad though," said Nellie, "to think that so many men out there fighting probably suffer the same mental tortures and injuries that can change their lives and personalities so much. Will our lives ever be as they once were?"

On 13 June 1944, a new terror weapon rained down over London; the flying bomb. It first landed in the East End of London, killing seven people. This bomb was the V-1 and became known as the doodle bug, or buzz bomb, due to the strange intermittent buzzing noise it emitted.

"Bloody hell! Three years after the blitz, we really began to think that this war would soon be over," cried Connie. "This bomb is more terrifying, because when it stops making a putt-putt noise like a motorbike, then it just falls out of the sky and no one knows where it will land."

"That's it, Nellie, I am so sorry but I must get out of London. Now I have the two kids, I can't stay here any longer."

"Where will you go?" asked Nellie.

"I will hopefully be able to go and stay with my aunt in Wales. Remember me telling you about her? At least, we should be safe there. Nellie, will you please consider coming with us?"

"No, as much as I will miss you all and I agree that it is the right decision for you, I feel that I must stay here in London and see if I can help in some way by working. With so few of our young men here, women have had to step up to the mark so that is what I must do. But I will feel so much better knowing that you and the children are safer away from London."

Both girls cried so much before Connie was due to depart. All the arrangements had been made and everything was packed up in the suitcase ready to go.

"You are doing the right thing, Connie, and the life for you and the children in Wales will be so much better for you all."

"I know I am and hopefully, we will be much safer in Wales. My aunt is so pleased to be having us stay with them on the small holding, but I will be constantly worried about you, what with all these wretched doodle-bugs raining down on London."

"Yes, but as I said before, you three are the only people left that I love and care for and knowing that you are safe means so much to me."

Nellie accompanied Connie and the kids to Kings Cross Station. At least Billy was walking, so with his reins on and baby Elizabeth in the pram, Nellie was able to place the two suitcases safely on the overhead racks above them.

"Uncle Jo will meet us at the station at the other end so I won't have to manage on my own, only the journey, and I feel sure that the children will sleep a good deal of the way."

Nellie gave the children a big hug and kiss then turned to Connie.

"Take good care of yourselves and write when you can, keeping me up-to-date on how these two rascals are doing."

"Why are you sad, Auntie Nellie?" asked Billy.

"That's because you are so lucky going on a train journey, how exciting will that be, and for now I have to stay here."

"Take care and hopefully in the not-too-distant future, we can be together again."

Nellie continued to wave until the train was out of sight.

Chapter 12

Nellie returned to her home and when she sat down to drink her tea, she had an overwhelming sense of loneliness; everyone that she had loved had gone. It dawned on her that she was totally alone here in London. Tears uninvited ran down her cheeks. Although of only 25 years of age, she suddenly felt old and that her youth was slipping by. Suddenly, the sirens sounded. Grabbing her blankets, torch and a book, she made her way out to the Anderson shelter.

She gave a wry smile. "Sod you, Hitler, you are the only one that hasn't deserted me."

Doodle bugs continued to rain down in London and the East End. Everyone was terrified when the sound of the engines cut out and waited for the bomb to drop. People would dive for cover and hope that this one did not have their name on it.

"Right then, gel, stop feeling sorry for yourself get up off your backside and do something for your country and don't let Hitler win this bloody war."

"Can you drive?" the officer asked.

"Yes, of course, and I have experience in driving heavy vehicles."

"Have you any nursing experience?"

"No but I have worked on the land with animals so I am not squeamish."

"Well, the ambulances are manned by a driver, and a rescue worker, so if you are happy, we will give you some basic life-saving training but we cannot train you for all eventualities and you will be seeing quite a bit of trauma. The other thing you need to understand is that, when the air raid sirens sound, that is when you go to work and not for shelter."

So, Nellie became an ambulance driver in and around the East of London, often needing to travel further into the London area. Initially, it was quite nerve-racking, especially when the distant sound of the V-1 came ever closer followed by the 12 seconds delay as the engine cut out, this was when no one knew where it would land and explode. People took shelter where they could and waited, wondering if this might be the last sound they heard.

No disappearing into the shelters now and taking cover. As soon as the bombs dropped, the ambulance drivers went out, because that was when most people needed saving. Most times, Nellie would be on call from six at night until eight the following morning, but she began to enjoy her work and the camaraderie. Many things were not pleasant and indeed very upsetting, but Nellie had to learn to deal with all situations, help those that she could and accept that some she could do nothing for, but she strived to get to the casualties and give as much assistance as she was able to so they would hopefully survive another day.

On one occasion, after working for eight months as an attendant, she went to a casualty who had been caught near an explosion. The man's injuries were difficult to assess as his face had been burned and covered in blood.

"What is your name, sir, my name is Nellie."

"Do not worry about me, lass, go and save someone else. I will be fine, I can wait for a while."

There was something about the resignation in his voice that touched Nellie. Usually, she did her job and tried to not allow herself to get emotionally involved otherwise she would not be able to continue in her work, but this man must have been in awful pain, but did not make any fuss.

Nellie informed the man that she would do everything she could to get him treated as soon as possible but also knowing that on this busy night, there would be many more similar cases. Applying a dressing to his face as best she could, they made their way to the nearest hospital. During the journey, the man told her that his name was Bernard but his friends called him Bernie.

Conversation stopped as they arrived at the hospital and after getting the casualty into A+E which was as usual heaving with casualties and never empty, Nellie and her crew mate were back out on the road, ready to attend more incidents and injuries.

Days later, when Nellie was off-duty, she returned to the hospital where she had taken Bernie. This was not something that she had done before as there were so many cases, so she learned to be able to move on and not allow herself to become emotionally involved, but for some reason this man had something that drew her to him.

It took a bit of time to track down where Bernie had been transferred to as there were so many in the hospital, requiring treatment. Nellie observed how tired many of the staff looked, the raining down during a spate of the V-l's indiscriminately killing and maiming people was obviously taking its toll.

Eventually, Bernie was tracked down and as Nellie made her way to his bed, she noticed that his eyes were bandaged over and cream had been applied to his burned face, so it was impossible to get an idea of what he looked like.

"Hello, Bernie," said Nellie.

"Who is that?" was the reply.

"It is Nellie, the ambulance driver, I picked you up after your accident."

Bernie did not converse much initially and appeared very low in spirits and mentally shut down.

Nellie for an unknown reason felt a connection to him and continued to visit on her days off.

"I am leaving in a couple of days," said Bernie on one of Nellie's visits. "They removed the dressings yesterday and told me that the damage to my eyes was so severe that I will now be blind for the rest of my life and that I now need to convalesce in a home as they need my bed. So I thank you for visiting me and giving up your spare time which has meant a great deal, but I shall be moving to Kent in a day or so."

"What about your family?" asked Nellie. "Would they not be able to take care of you?"

With this, Bernie choked back his emotions and did not reply straight away. After what seemed an age, Bernie explained that he had come home on leave to his wife and two children only to find out that they had sustained a direct hit by a doodle bug on their home and all were killed instantly. "So, I don't have anyone and in fact, although I am grateful to you, I wish that I had been killed that night instead of just being blinded. I have no interest in what happens to me now, I have lost everything and have no desire to carry on."

Nellie could completely empathise with this comment and just said that there is always something to live for, even if at the time it cannot be seen.

"Right then, young man, I have spoken to the doctor and you are coming home with me to recuperate."

"No, Nellie, I could not do that, it would not be fair on you. Remember, I am blind and will be a burden."

"Not at all, you can have the downstairs parlour for your bedroom, so I will not accept any arguments. Anyway, Bernie, like you I do not have anyone either so we can be company for one another."

"One thing I would ask of you, Nellie," asked Bernie, "would you help me to write a letter to my wife's family to let them know of their loss?"

Chapter 13

Initially, it was a lot harder than Nellie had first imagined it would be, but having company and the sound of someone else in the house was somehow comforting. Bernie continued to have regular checks at the local hospital, and eventually all the dressings were removed.

"Hey, you are not such a bad looker," laughed Nellie one day after she had shaven the stubble off his face.

Bernie was older than Nellie by 15 years, his face was now scarred from the explosion but he still retained his good looks.

Although they were building a very good friendship with lots of banter, Bernie would often go quite and withdrawn and Nellie knew that although his facial scars were healing, his emotional ones were deep. He still did not speak of his loss or much at all about his past, so Nellie just talked about the here and now when they had moments together.

Gradually, Bernie was able to find his way around the downstairs of Nellie's house and negotiate going out to the outside toilet. He also enjoyed sitting in the small garden listening to the chickens as they pecked away at the ground.

"I cannot thank you enough for all that you have done for me, Nellie, but now that I have recovered as much as I ever will, I feel that I have imposed long enough and I will try and find somewhere else to live."

"Have you had enough of my company then, you ungrateful sod?" laughed Nellie. "I enjoy having you here. I so miss my close friend and her children, it is nice not to be alone. Please stay for as long as you wish unless there is somewhere else you need to be."

"No," replied Bernie, "there is nowhere." Bernie said these few words in such a way that Nellie was grateful that he could not see the tears roll down her cheeks as she felt his pain, because it so reflected her own.

"One day, this bloody war will be over and maybe we can all start to rebuild our lives," replied Nellie.

Once Bernie was able to find his way around the downstairs of the house and able to manage using the small cooker to make drinks and food, Nellie felt comfortable in returning to work.

"Anyone seeing you around the house and negotiating the steps down into the kitchen would not know that you could not see."

"Just so long as nothing is left on the floor or furniture moved, then I feel in my mind that I can see my way around. I am happy to take myself out into the garden and sit and talk to the chickens," replied Bernie. "Thank you again, Nellie, for giving me this opportunity to try and enjoy life again. It's funny, now I am unable to see I feel that I use my other senses more. I listen to the birds singing in the tree outside, I hear the milkman coming down the street early in the morning, with the bottles rattling in their crates. The rag and bone man calling out for any old wares along with the sound of the horses' hooves on the tarmac. Sometimes, I can hear women chatting and gossiping outside, though I cannot make out what they are saying, just the conversation which turns to whispers. The best sound of all and yet the most painful is the sound of the children playing in the street after school, listening to the laughter and the squabbles before their mothers call them in for their tea. So, Nellie, I am learning to accept that however hard and however we do it, life must go on."

Nellie felt that it was a move forward and that one day, the deep pain may start to rise giving him the chance to talk and share, but she was happy that this was at least a start.

Doodle bugs continued to rain down causing so much injury, death and pain. Because no one knew where they would land; all people could do when the sound of the engine stopped was to take cover and pray.

Nellie would go into the areas recently bombed, driving through areas of burning buildings to attend to the injured. Many times, the only thing she could do would be to hold someone's hand so that they did not feel alone at the end. She tried hard to get to the casualties quickly and transferred to the nearest hospital for treatment. Nellie found that there were many funny moments as well, like the time an elderly gentleman had been seen scrabbling around on all fours calling out, On checking, he had not been injured by a recent explosion, it transpired that he had gone out to the outside loo. As a doodle bug sounded nearby, he had run out towards his shelter leaving his pyjama bottoms around his ankles and as he slipped and fell, his top set of false teeth flew out. He was looking for them. No one knew if they were ever found.

Another occasion after an explosion another gentleman was found running in the street calling out that he was blind.

What had actually happened was that the explosion had been very close by, causing all the windows of his house to blow outwards and the walls to move, which in turn pulled the curtain pole that was hanging at the front door to fall, wrapping the curtains around his body tightly, so not only could he not see, but he was also tightly cocooned by the fabric and unable to free himself. Frightening though it must have been for him at the time, it did give many neighbours a good well-needed laugh.

One morning, a letter arrived from Connie.

Dearest Nellie

I hope that all is well with you and that things are not as bad as we hear on the radio about London, what with the new bombs, although we hear that anti-aircraft often manage to shoot them down before they reach London, I do hope that this is so and that you remain safe.

Life here is so much better for the kids, they are both doing so well and they have much more freedom to roam in the fields and fresh air. Billy is now running around like a mad thing and loves nothing better than helping to collect the eggs in the morning from the hen house. The house although not large is very cosy and the views from the hill tops remind me of my childhood in Ireland. We have our own room and me and the kids sleep in the one bed. There is a spare box room, but I prefer to have the children in with me. Downstairs, there is a front room with an open fire and off of the kitchen a small area large enough for a table and chairs where we all sit and eat. Aunt Margaret often gets Billy to sit at the table with her and she has shown him how to shell the peas that have been grown in the small vegetable garden that Uncle Roy manages.

Mind you, there are as many pods in the bowl as peas, but still it keeps Billy quiet. Elizabeth now has three teeth and when we prop her up in a chair, she laughs away as Billy makes faces at her or interacts with her, you will notice a lot of changes in them by the time you next meet.

I do miss you though and the busy life in London that we once knew. Often I sit and look back to when we first met and the fun we had, but I have to say living here you would almost not know that a war was going on. Rationing although we have it here, we are able to eat better as lots of things are grown locally and eggs are not rationed like in London.

My aunt and uncle are lovely people but are old now, so I do miss the company of younger people. Here in the small village there is not much to do, we have a small shop that sells all the basics and for entertainment there is always the local gossip, or on a couple of occasions I have gone with my aunt to the small village hall and played bingo. Mind you, Nellie, you would be proud of me, I have made the kids some clothes out of some old curtains that my aunt had; they may not be anywhere near as good as what you make but they do. It is just as well Billy is as young as he is as the fabric is very floral!

How are things with you, please write now you have the address to contact me, I would love to hear your news and Billy often asks where Auntie Nellie is, so I would be able to tell him what you are up to.

Please take good care of yourself and as I have said before, you know that you would be very welcome to come out here to live until the war is over.

All our love, Connie, Billy and Elizabeth. XXXX

Nellie put the letter down on the table and shed a few tears. How she missed her family, because that is how she saw them now, as it was all she had. Nellie also had a nagging fear that because Connie's life was more settled and especially better for the children, would they ever come back?

"Right, tea break over, there is work to be done, the war cannot go on for ever and as it is the doodle bugs are far fewer lately." Nellie then sat herself at her small table and wrote a reply letter to Connie, telling her all about her lodger Bernie and her work in the ambulance service.

One evening, whilst Nellie and Bernie sat listening to the radio on which Glen Miller and his band were playing, Nellie dared to ask about his past and if he wanted to talk. Nellie was amazed that Bernie finally was able to discuss a little about his lost family and her heart went out to him as he cried.

"I am so sorry, Nellie, to be babbling like a baby in front of you," he said as he wiped away the tears from his cheeks.

"Don't be so daft," she replied, "you need to release some of that heartache that you are carrying." Nellie just sat and allowed him to talk and let it all flow without interruption.

It transpired that his family had returned home to Aldrich where they lived after living in the West country due to the earlier heavy bombing, which appeared to have stopped. Bernie did not want them to return until peace had been declared, but his wife was so homesick that she made the fatal decision. Apparently, they had only been back a short time when the house and others took a direct hit from the buzz bomb and his wife and two daughters were killed instantly. Bernie explained that he was making his way home on leave so he did not know anything until he arrived back.

"The only thing that consoles me is the fact that they would not have known a thing, it would have been instant, but I just wish that Maureen had waited as I had wanted her to."

Nellie just sat and listened, she knew only too well that feeling. She reflected back to when she had found her beloved grandparents' house completely wiped out.

Nellie then got up and did what the English did best in times like this, she went and made them a cup of tea.

Later that evening, Bernie excused himself as he headed to the back door to go to the outside toilet.

"Bernie?" called out Nellie. "Don't forget to take the candle, it's dark outside," to which they both burst into laughter.

"You daft cow, it makes no difference to me as I am bloody blind anyway."

In October 1944, Allied forces in France overran the last V-1 launch site in range of Britain and the bombing attacks suddenly stopped just as swiftly as they had begun.

After the bombing stopped, the capital's one million evacuees returned home; women, children and the elderly all gradually came home again.

On 8 May 1945, a public holiday was declared, VE Day and celebrations that the war in Europe was finally over began.

Nellie was overjoyed that Connie returned back to London to join in the celebrations.

"I am sorry that I have not brought the children with me, but I decided it would be better for them to remain in the country with my aunt and uncle for now and after the celebrations, I will return back to Wales for a while, just until things are totally settled again."

Nellie's heart skipped a beat; this was what she had feared but now was not the time to discuss. It was now time to PARTY along with thousands of others in celebrating the end of the war; although some were still out fighting in other areas of the world, the war was not over for them for a while.

Connie and Bernie got on really well. They chatted away like they had known one another for years and Nellie observed that Bernie's general demeanour was improving. He had gradually started to take more interest in life, also in his own appearance. No longer would he go for days unshaven and disinterested in how he looked.

"He is a bit of all right," said Connie when they were alone.

Bernie had taken himself off to his room. "Let you girls catch up and chat privately, I will go and listen to the radio and leave you in peace."

Nellie told Connie the circumstances of how they met.

"How old were his daughters?" asked Connie.

"I believe one was 12 years and the younger girl 10."

"Oh, what a tragedy. If only she had waited another few months, things would have been so different, but then so many lives have been lost in this wretched war that really there have been no winners," replied Connie.

"Anyway, how is it with you two?" smiled Connie. "He is nice, no one would know that he was blind the way he moves around the house, I certainly would not kick him out of my bed."

"It is not like that, we are just good friends. He has had so much mental anguish to cope with that I don't think any improper thoughts would have entered his head. Mind you, I have to admit that as time has gone by and he is slowly healing that I have become very fond of him and I am seeing him in a different light."

Bernie was losing that tortured look and his face was beginning to soften, showing a handsome strong-jawed look, his unseeing eyes were brown in colour but had quite a lot of scarring from the burns around his eyes and face. He was about 6ft in height and a good strong build; in fact, now that Connie had pointed it out to Nellie, she had to agree that although older, he had made a good companion and easy company.

Rationing was still very much in force and would be for some time, but street parties were held to celebrate the end of what had been a long war. Streets were lined with tables and chairs, union jack flags were everywhere, people provided food and everyone came together, the children and adults had a marvellous time and joined in the celebrations. Nellie persuaded Bernie to come out and join in. At first, he was reluctant but eventually he relented under the pressure from both Nellie and Connie and in fact, he really enjoyed the atmosphere and the sounds of people and children having fun. Nellie kept an eye on him and now and then could sense that his thoughts were elsewhere, so after a while, she would go up to him and just give his hand a gentle touch, to let him know that she was there and she fully understood.

Bernie declined the offer to accompany the girls up to London to Trafalgar square to join in the celebrations.

"No, thank you so much for asking me, but I will only be a hindrance. You girls go and have a wonderful time, you really deserve to let your hair down. I really enjoyed the street party and that is good enough for me, but again, bless you for inviting me."

Nellie and Connie dressed up in the best dresses they could muster.

"I knew that one day we would get the chance to wear some of Mary's clothes and no better way than now celebrating the end of the war. We can imagine that she is here with us in spirit," smiled Connie.

With a few alterations made by Nellie, they looked a treat. Makeup applied and hair done up, they were ready to celebrate. As they went to go out the front door, Bernie was already there.

"Gave a great evening, girls." Then as Nellie was about to go, he pulled her to one side and gave her a gentle, soft kiss on her cheek and said, "Be safe."

During the celebrations, crowds of over a million were in London and the atmosphere was fantastic. Everyone was having a great time, total strangers giving one another a hug or a kiss. For the first time in a long while, people could relax and let their hair down. It was rumoured the Royal Princesses Elizabeth and Margaret were out amongst the people enjoying the party.

Crowds massed in Trafalgar Square then made their way up the Mall to Buckingham Palace, where on the balcony King George, Queen Elizabeth along with Winston Churchill appeared on the balcony waving to the crowds.

After all the celebrations, Connie returned to Wales and her children with the promise that she would return to London "when things are settled".

One day, a month or two after VE Day, a letter arrived addressed to Bernie.

"It is from my in-laws. As you can imagine, they were devastated to hear the news of their daughter and granddaughters, but they want me to go and live with them in Hampshire. My father-in-law runs a small company and feels sure that he can offer me a position even with my disabilities."

Nellie was not sure if she was happy or not with this news.

"It would be for the best, Nellie. I cannot thank you enough for all that you have done for me. You gave me a reason to carry on living in my darkest days, but the war is now over, thank god, and you need to start a new life for yourself. I would only be a burden and hold you back, so please understand, Nellie, that it is for the best. They are nice people, my in-laws, and at least I will feel more of a man again if I can start to earn a living."

"I feel that everyone eventually leaves me, what is it about me that I keep losing people I am so fond of?" cried Nellie.

"You will not lose me, Nellie. I promise you that I will keep in touch. Anyway, you will soon have your hands full when Connie and the children return."

Bernie left a few weeks later, accompanied by his father-in-law. Promises were made to keep in touch and that now was the time to look forward and not back.

"Oh well, my beloved house," said Nellie as she once again sat in the empty house alone, "at least you and me are still together."

Chapter 14

At long last, the war time rationing had finally ended by 1953. Although shortages continued for several years after the war, people were beginning to feel more positive about the future.

"Has anyone got a good recipe for a meat pie, it's been so bleedin' long since I made one I have forgotten how. I have a fancy to make my Burt a meat pie with chips for dinner tonight."

"Oh yeh, what are you after then?" called out one of the women on the shop floor.

"Not what you're thinking, that's for sure, it ain't his birthday yet."

"Well, I reckon that your old man may think that his luck's in with a slap up meal like that put in from of him."

"Well thinking he might get something ain't the same as getting it."

All the women working on the shop floor started to laugh as they worked away on their sewing machines.

Betty Cox was a very popular woman with a larger-than-life personality, a natural comedian with a heart of gold deep down, but cross her and she was a force to be reckoned with.

Nellie had left the ambulance service after the war had ended. She tentatively considered training as a nurse, but her first love was making and altering clothes, which was handy as during the war time when everyone had to make do and mend, Nellie was able to fashion and alter clothes from old garments, so when a position came up at the Singer sewing factory in East London, Nellie went along to see if she could obtain a position there. The manager explained that during war time, the women made service uniforms as part of the war effort. Today, the women were again making garments to be sold up in the West End shops as they did in the pre-war days. Many of the factory women were the same ones who had been there before and during the war and would tell many a hair-raising tale of the bombings, but also many stories about the fun that they had.

"This was our finishing school," said Betty one day, a real East Ender with very colourful language to match.

"If they don't like the way I talk, well then, that's tough bleedin' luck," she laughed.

Nellie really enjoyed working with these high-spirited ladies and certainly learned a thing or two. She thought that she had become quite worldly during war time, but these ladies took it to a whole new level. They enjoyed life and dealt with whatever was thrown at them and like herself, many had lost loved ones during wartime.

"Well, gel, the way I sees it, we can't change what's past, so we just has to keep going forward. Never forget those poor souls that we have lost, but as they say, life goes on. Here I tell you what, come down the pub with us one night and let your hair down, but take care it's not your smalls as there are some randy old buggers out there."

To this, many of the older ladies all gave a knowing nod.

"I will take you up on that offer," said Nellie. "I could really do with a night out and I am sure that with you lot, it is sure to be interesting!"

Nellie kept in touch with Connie and had visited them in Wales on a couple of occasions. the children were now both at the local school and growing up fast and suited living the country life. They went down to the beach regularly as it was within walking distance. Billy could now swim and Elizabeth would not be long as she had no fear of water. Connie was also looking well and they all looked slightly tanned.

"All this fresh air and good food agrees with you, look at the colour in your cheeks."

"Thank you, Nellie, I do feel that leaving London when I did was absolutely the right thing to do, but now that the kids are off to school all day, I do get lonely.

"Oh, I get on very well with my aunt and uncle and I am so grateful for them taking us in and for such a long time, but they are now old and like to go to bed early so I do get very lonely here. There really isn't much to do, even less in the long dark winter months. I often sit and reflect back over my life and living in London."

"Is there nowhere that you can go in the evening and get to meet other people? What about some of the other mums, don't they invite you 'round to them?"

"Most still have their husbands, so in the evenings they are indoors looking after the kids while the husbands go out to the local pub. Most of the women are friendly, but it is not like the East End."

When Nellie returned home to London, she did worry about Connie and how her young life was possibly slipping by being so isolated. She knew that it was for the children but she also had to think about herself as well. Nellie thought of how Connie would love the nights out in the pub with the ladies she worked with, singing well-known songs as they all drank more and the conversations would become more bawdy and near the mark as the evenings went on, Nellie just loved the now regular evenings in their company and she knew that Connie would as well.

During their working day, the women often sang. One would start out humming a tune followed by another, then in no time at all a full blown singing session would break out drowning the sounds of the sewing machines. Some of the ladies were war-hardened and quite gruff in their manner, but that was because the East end of London was so badly affected during the war they needed to be tough and resilient. But as tough as they appeared and you would not wish to fall out with some of them, they all had hearts of gold and would give you their last penny if it was needed. Within the factory, there was a real camaraderie and although often a row between two women might break out, when it was time to go home at the end of the day, all was usually forgotten.

Out of the blue one morning, a letter come through the post addressed to Nellie.

Hello, Nellie,

I have been trying to locate Connie for some time now, letters that I have sent to her previous address have been returned, so I found your address and hoped that you are still in contact with her.

Please find enclosed a letter for Connie in the hopes that you will be able to forward it, it is important for me to get hold of her.

Thank you.
Pete.

"Well, that was pretty short and sweet and what a turn up for the books, so he is still alive then the ba----d. I wonder what he wants from Connie now after all these years. Oh well, I will get this in the post a bit sharp."

Days later, a letter came and Nellie recognised it as Connie's writing.

Dear Nellie,

Thank you for forwarding the letter from Pete. I was, like you, surprised to receive it, but it turns out that he has got his life back together now and has met someone else who he wishes to marry, so he wants a divorce. Oh Nellie, it's not that he has found someone else or the divorce, to be honest I couldn't give a shit. But he never once asked about his son Billie and he does not even know that he has a daughter. Needless to say, I did not even mention them, they are better off thinking that he died in the war! I know that seems cruel but better that than having a dad that doesn't care or want to know them.

I am seriously thinking of coming back to London now. I know that my aunt and uncle will miss us, especially the kids, but am feeling so lonely and when I read your letters and the fun you seem to be having with your work mates, I feel that I am missing out on life. Please could you look out for a place preferably near to you that I may rent? Lots of love from me and the kids.

Connie.

Within a few months, Connie was as good as her word and she and the children returned. Nellie met them at Plaistow station after their long journey. Hugs, kisses and tears of joy at being re-united.

"You looked tired, Connie. Let's get you home and settled with a nice cup of tea, some food in your bellies and a good night's sleep will soon sort you out."

Nellie's house only had the two bedrooms upstairs so it was arranged that Connie and Elizabeth would share the double-bed in the back bedroom and Billy would sleep downstairs in the parlour on a put-up bed. Nellie also had a surprise for Connie and the children. She had decided that with the money that Mary had left in her will, she was able to buy the house outright and add an extension that was turned into a bathroom and indoor toilet.

"How luxurious," smiled Connie when she saw it. "No going outside in the freezing cold with a lamp anymore."

The children also loved it, the idea of not having to sit in the old tin bath in front of the fire. Although it was warm and cosy by the fire, it was not very private.

Initially, they lived with Nellie until a suitable place nearby was found. Billy was now almost 11 years old and Elizabeth 9 years; it took a little while to adjust to life in a London street with its rows of terraced houses after being so free in the country, but once they had made a few friends, they soon settled as children tend to adapt very quickly. The street, which by now was completely different to when Nellie first moved in had quite a few young families with their children. Most of the mums encouraged the kids to go and play outside with the others and 'not get under their feet' so the street became a playground for the youngsters. Chalk marks were always seen on the pavements where the girls would play hopscotch, boys would put jumpers down on the road surface to act as goal posts while they played football and the street during school holidays and weekends would be full of kids playing and arguing. Mums would often go out and turn the skipping ropes for the girls and often would tuck their dresses into their knickers and have a go themselves. Outside one of the houses was a Victorian street lamp that had a small iron bar sticking out where once the lamplighter would rest his ladder, the kids now had a rope tied around this bar and would swing 'round the pole hanging on the rope, get the timing wrong and it sure did hurt as your body banged against the cast iron lamp.

"What have you done now?" said Connie as Billy came in crying with blood on his knees and chin.

"He was swinging on the rope hanging from the lamp post and fell off," explained young Lizzie as she was now nicknamed in the street.

As Elizabeth was getting older, she took it upon herself to look after and boss around her older brother. She was becoming tougher now that she was having to hold her own with the bigger children, but it was lovely to see how they all got on and generally played together. Because the street had a dead end with just an alleyway cutting through to the next street, it was perfectly safe for the kids to play. Also there were very few vehicles that came down, only the coal man had a lorry, the milkman had a float and the rag and bone man would come down on a horse and cart, which after he left the kids would run out and shovel up the manure for their dad's garden or some were lucky enough to have an allotment nearby.

Life was settling down into a rhythm and although they continued to look for a suitable place for Connie and the children, Nellie was more than happy to have them stay with her. It was wonderful to have the sound of voices laughing and arguing, fighting and playing. The house had been so quiet for so long that it was now a noisy home, but it was now a home not just a house.

Nellie and Connie enjoyed a few nights out with the women whilst a neighbours daughter Jenny would look after the kids for a bit of pocket money. As Nellie suspected, Connie really enjoyed herself and where initially some of the ripe language shocked her, she was now able to join in as good as the rest of them, saving it only for when they were out and not in front of the kids.

"Why don't you two and the kids come with us hop picking later in the year?" said Betty one day.

Betty was not a tall lady, well-rounded she would describe herself as, she had not one but a couple of chins, which would wobble when she laughed. Her ample breasts came 'round the corner before she did which were slightly more contained when she wore her crossover apron, which unless going out was worn pretty much all the time. A head scarf with one or two rollers at the front was pretty much a uniform standard for many of the women, that along with a fag hanging out of their mouths when not sewing was another addition to the uniform.

"Sounds like it might be fun to have a working holiday hop picking and earn a few bob, what do you think, Nellie?" asked Connie.

Betty jumped in on the conversation. "It can be bloody hard work and your fingers often get sore, but the more you pick the more you earn and in the evenings when the kids are tucked up in bed and asleep, we sit and have a natter or nip to the local for a drink."

So the two women agreed that they would go when it was the right time of the year.

Both Nellie and Connie still had a little money left from what Mary had left them, but both had tucked it away 'for a rainy day'.

"How do you fancy just us two going down the road to our local on Saturday night? We have not been out for some time now. I am sure that young Jenny will mind the kids," suggested Nellie.

So come Saturday, the two women rolled up their hair in the morning and left the rollers in for the day. That evening, they got themselves ready to go out.

"This takes me back to earlier years when we lived at Mary's before the war and the three of us would get ready to go out. I wonder whatever happened to Grace."

Makeup on and their hair brushed out, both women looked lovely.

"Wow, Mum, you do look smashing and so do you, Aunt Nell," commented Billy as they got ready to leave.

"Now you both be good for Jenny and we will see you in the morning."

Both Connie and Nellie gave the kids a kiss.

"You know where we are if you need us," Connie said to the young girl.

"Mum's only a few doors away if I need help," replied Jenny. "You both go and have a good time."

The Red Lion on a Saturday night was always lively, especially once the beer started to flow. Old Mrs Martin was there again on the piano where she would remain for the whole evening, playing popular songs (so long as she was supplied with her glass of stout). Tom Smith was another regular that would often accompany the piano by playing the spoons against his thigh. Most of the people in the pub would sing along and often songs that had helped them through the war years, many a tear would be shed in remembrance. Later on in the evening, the fish man would often come into the pub holding up a large basket which contained a variety of shell fish, cockles, mussels and jellied eels. Outside on his stall, salt, vinegar and dry bread was available. Customers were always pleased to see him, especially after having a few drinks and by the time he left the pub, there was not much left in his basket.

The singing and chatter got louder and louder as the evening wore on and the yarn spinning tales grew longer. Often outside the pubs, kids would be eating bags of crisps with a bottle of pop and there they would stay until their parents came out again, often quite late.

"It is such a shame that so many young men were lost in the war, there are none in the pub tonight. Everyone appears middle to old age," moaned Connie.

"I know, I think that now there are more women than men in this country. It is so sad, so many losses, but we would need to go up West if we want to meet any young men."

"Perhaps one evening on a weekend we can do that, get on a train and have a night out. For now, we had better get home so that young Jenny can get home, we don't want her mother after us," replied Connie.

Life continued as usual, the women at work would often discuss the previous night's activities and have a good old gossip generally about what someone had been seen getting up to; nothing seemed to be missed by these eagle-eyed women. Colourful language was compulsory in their discussions, but Nellie loved it there. Sometimes, she would get a bit frustrated sewing the same garments. She craved the opportunity to expand her own designs, but these garments were to be sold in London and the bosses knew what was selling best at the time.

"Why don't you make some outfits at home then you can do your own designs and see if you can sell them, even if you just advertise in the local shop," suggested Connie one day. "We would need to find out where you can buy the fabric, but there are many places in the East End where I am sure you can get it."

"Maybe one day, I might give it a go, but I do enjoy the company of those women at work, so I would need to be working in the evenings and weekends."

"Here Nellie," called out Betty one day. "Met any nice fellas yet?"

"Chance would be a fine thing," Nellie shouted back.

"Well, my nephew is single, not a bad looker and around your age. He may not be the sharpest tool in the box, but he has a kind nature, a bit like myself really."

To this, the laughter rang out from all the women almost drowning out the sounds of the machines.

"Here I must tell you gels, my Bert got a bit amorous last night when he came in from the pub, so I lets him fink that he was on to a good thing but told him to freshen up first as he stank of beer. Well, I heard him coming up the stairs so I waited, the there was an almighty crash followed by a few swear words, then nothing. I laid there for a while and thought I had best get up and see what the old bugger had done. There he was at the top of the landing, trousers 'round his ankles asleep on the floor, it would appear that as he had come up the stairs, his trousers had fallen down, he tripped and there he was stretched out."

"Jesus, Betty! He could have been dead or unconscious."

"Na, he was snoring as usual, so I threw a blanket on him and went back to bed. I thought I would check him in the morning."

"Did you not just say that you had a kind nature, Betty?" shouted out one the ladies.

Another called out, "So there was no night of passion then?"

Betty replied, "The only passion I get is when he rolls on, rolls off, gives a fart then snores, loves young dream aye. See what ya got to look forward to, Nellie."

Again laughter rang out in the room. Nellie really enjoyed the ladies' down-to-earth banter, yet most of them had a heart of gold and prepared to help anyone out, even if they themselves were short.

"There is a letter for you on the table, Connie, it looks official," said Nellie one morning in late summer.

"It's from the council, a house has just become available. It's a two bedroom in East Ham, they advise me to go and view it as there is a lot of people that need rehousing. What do you think, Nellie?"

"What was the house like?" asked Nellie the next day. She wanted to go with Connie to see it, but the factory could not spare both girls at such short notice.

"It was OK, but not as nice as this one. It was in a long street with rows of houses, the road was a main one, the garden was so small it was almost non-existent and it required a lot of repair work and it was certainly in need of redecorating, but Nellie, the kids would have to change schools and now they are so settled here and have so many friends I would hate to have to upset them but equally I feel that you now need your own space especially as the kids are getting older."

"Don't give it another thought, I love having you all here. The house is more homely with a bit of noise and I would miss you all, so if it does not feel right, then do not move. Let another family have it."

So Connie declined the house and was told that she may not get the offer of another for a long time, if ever.

"I have a surprise for you all in the parlour," said Nellie one day when the kids returned from school.

"What is it?" the excited children asked.

Nellie had taken a day off from work and took herself off to do some shopping specifically to purchase the item.

"Wait until Mummy comes in then we can all go and see."

"Mum, hurry up and get your coat off, we have been waiting so long for you. Auntie Nellie has a surprise and we were not allowed to see until you came in."

"Give me a chance to catch my breath then." Connie was assisted out of her coat and ushered along to the parlour.

As Nellie opened the door to the room, the two children and Connie stopped and stared. There in the corner stood a television, it was a small screen contained in a cabinet.

"What is it?" exclaimed Lizzie.

"Don't you know?" said Billy with a huge smile on his face and proudly announced to his young sister that it was a box that showed pictures that moved; 'a television'.

Nellie switched it on and they all sat and waited for what seemed an age as it warmed up.

"What's it supposed to do?" asked Lizzie.

"Just wait and see," answered Nellie.

"Wow!"

Gradually, a black and white picture appeared and they all sat and looked at the screen.

"I believe that they have programs at certain times of the day, especially for children."

So for a short time each day, the children were allowed to watch some programs on the television. The women found that this was also a great way to bribe the children if they needed to. Billy loved the likes of 'The Lone Ranger' and 'Rin Tin Tin', whereas Elizabeth enjoyed programs such as 'Lassie' and 'Popeye'. The children would sit quietly on the sofa and wait for their favourites to be shown.

"Whatever possessed you to buy that?" asked Connie. "It must have cost a fortune."

"Well, I still have a little money from the sale of Mary's house, so why not, we will all get some enjoyment out of it, I am sure, especially with the nights drawing in."

"We will be the poshest kids in the school," crowed Billy as they sat and watched children's hour together.

"That money was for you, Nellie," said Connie.

"Look, I am never going to have kids of my own, but Billy and Lizzie are as good as mine, so let me spoil them if I want to."

"Nellie, I don't know if I have ever told you, but I do love you. You are the closest that I have ever been to anyone and we have lived and shared some pretty rotten times, but we have made it through them. Now I just wish you could meet someone special again to share your life with because, lady, you deserve it, you are one in a million."

"Thank you, Connie, but the feeling is mutual. We have had some tough experiences to face, but I tell you what, if having a lover like Betty describes her husband's bedroom activities, I think I would rather give it a miss."

Both women howled with laughter.

Nellie and Connie declined the offer of hop picking when the time came, but promised that they would give it some thought for the following year. Instead, they took the children for a week's holiday to Southend-on-Sea. Between them, they could afford to stay in a B&B near the sea front.

"Where are we going?" asked the excited children. Their mother had their suitcases packed, but up until now had not said a word to them as she wanted to keep it as a surprise until the last moment.

"Tomorrow morning, we will need to get up early as we will be getting the train to the seaside for a holiday."

"Hooray! Are we going back to where we used to live with Granny and Granddad?"

Although they were Connie's aunt and uncle, the children always referred to them as their grandparents.

"No, we are not going that far but we do need to catch a train to get there."

Connie felt a pang of guilt, she had not kept in regular contact with her aunt and uncle since leaving Wales. They were frail enough when she last saw them so promising herself that she would write to them sooner rather than later, she attempted to settle two excited children down for the night. Eventually, silence came from upstairs. Connie popped up to see them and sure enough they were both sound asleep.

"Thank goodness they have finally settled; otherwise, we would have had two very grumpy, tired kids to cope with."

"Well, they can always sleep on the train, I am ready for my bed as well if you don't mind," said Nellie. "Long day tomorrow, night night."

Billy and Lizzie were awake early. After wiping the sleep from their eyes, they remembered that they were off on their holidays and the excitement rose again. The walk to Plaistow station was roughly 25 mins but today, the walk seemed to be much quicker as they all chatted about what they would like to do on holiday.

"Can we buy some buckets and spades and make sand castles?" asked Lizzie.

"I am sure we can," laughed Connie.

Lizzie slept for a good deal of the journey from Liverpool Street to Southend, but Billy enjoyed the scenery which changed from busy city to semi-rural.

"I have been thinking for some time now that we could one day go up to Norfolk to where I worked on the farm during the war. It would be nice to see how they all are. I am sure that we may find somewhere to stay for a night or two. It was a lovely county, albeit hard work, but fun too."

"Do you regret not going back sooner? You might have seen the American again," asked Connie as she noticed that Nellie had a fleetingly sad look on her face.

"I suppose if I am honest, yes, I began to become very fond of him and in time we could have grown very close, but he was not mine to have. Anyway, enough of that. Let's get ready as I think we are near the station."

They arrived at the B&B and were shown to their rooms by a small but very business-like lady who introduced herself as Mrs Cox. The rooms were not exactly spacious, basic but very clean. Luckily, they both had sea views and when the windows were opened. the smell of salt in the air felt wonderful. Mrs Cox explained the rules of the house then left them to settle down. There was one bathroom upstairs and downstairs to be shared by all the guests, but fortunately, there never appeared to be a queue.

"I am so glad that I now have a look inside the house and that I can call it my own, thanks to Mary."

"I never liked to ask, Nellie, but did you get the house for a fair price?"

"I told the old bugger that because I had been a good tenant for many years and that there was some obvious damage to the property during the war, he should consider letting me have it for a fair price and he did. I think that he had a few damaged houses from the war that possibly needed some repairs or rebuilding, having a bit of cash would help him out to no end."

"You never said that you had been damaged from the bombs?"

"That's because I didn't, I was luckier than many nearby. There have been a few cracks appearing, but I do not think that they are structural."

"You crafty cow, did he not check?"

Lucky for them the weather remained warm, so most days were spent sitting on the beach and letting the kids make sand castles. They would walk along the sea front and as a treat have ice cream or even a candy floss. They made flags out of the lolly sticks and pieces of paper. Often in the evenings, the children coloured in pictures on the flags with their crayons and use them the next day on their castles. Nellie and Billy formed a team against Connie and Lizzie to see who could build the largest and fanciest castle. Some of the days, the children would join others sitting on their chairs in front of a red and white small tent where they would be entertained by Punch and Judy. The cries of the children calling out for the policeman and generally joining in and taking it all very seriously as Judy would hit Punch or vice versa. Connie and Nellie just smiled, to see the children having so much fun did them the world of good too. This would then be followed up by ice creams all 'round. When the kids were occupied, the women would stretch out their towels and soak up the sun and inhale the salty fragrance of the sea air. By evening, everyone would be hungry and sleepy, often the treat would be a bag of fish and chips. They always tasted so much better when wrapped up in old newspapers and sprinkled with salt and vinegar. Mavis, the landlady of the B&B, bustled and fussed around but she ran her business with strict morals and cleanliness.

Initially, the women were concerned that she may not approve too much of having young kids in her establishment. Although they were well-behaved whilst inside the house, once out in the fresh sea air they were like wild things. As the week wore on, they all got on very well together and the children would often be given an extra treat at tea time of a cake or something that Mavis had made earlier in the day. No one needed any rocking off to sleep at night time, sleep came easy after a day in the fresh sea air, not even any rowdy revellers coming out from the pubs could disturb their slumbers.

The following day would be their last and Nellie went as usual along to the beach with Connie and the kids, but later that afternoon before returning to the guest house, Nellie exclaimed that she wanted to go for a walk alone.

"Is everything all right?" asked Connie.

"Yes, but I would just like to be alone for a while."

"Oh god, I completely forgot that this is where you and Tommy spent your honeymoon, oh how thoughtless of me. I am so sorry Nellie."

"Where is Aunty Nellie going?" called the kids as they saw her walking away on her own. "Can we go with her?"

"No, sometimes grownups like to have some time on their own for a while. You stay here with me for a bit longer then we will go back for tea."

Nellie walked along the sea front and revisited the places that she remembered her and Tommy going to, inhaling the fragrance of the salt and sea weed, listening to the waves as they rolled onto the sand, hearing the voices of laughter and chatter as people walked along the front. At the time with Tommy, it all added to the feeling of happiness and love; now it only made her feel lonely.

"Oh Tommy, it feels like a lifetime ago, such a lot has happened since we were here on our honeymoon. I miss you so much, such a waste of yours and so many others' lives. How I long to feel your touch and see your face again," Nellie continued to just walk for a long time remembering the past and wondering how different her life may have been had the war not intervened.

It was quite late when she returned to the B&B. She was so deep in thought that she had not realised the time.

"Bloody hell, Nellie!" exclaimed Connie. "I was beginning to get worried, we thought that we may need to send out a search party."

"Here you are, sit yourself down and have this hot cup of tea. I am just warming up your dinner then I will bring it in for you," said Mavis.

"That is so kind of you, I truly did not realise that it was so late. Have the kids gone to bed?"

"They were so tired that they just about kept their eyes open to eat their dinner. They said to give you a goodnight kiss," replied Connie.

That night alone in her room, Nellie for the first time in a long while cried herself to sleep.

The journey home again after such a wonderful week seemed to take less time than the journey up, but as the children slept, Nellie looked at them with their suntanned faces and thanked Mary for leaving them the money to be able to afford to give the children such a treat.

You would have loved them, Mary, they are so good. Life can be cruel and yours was taken too soon as were many others, but you with your kind heart will never be forgotten.

The next thing Nellie heard was the whistle of the station master as they pulled back in to Liverpool Street Station again.

"Have you written your letters to Father Christmas yet?" asked Nellie to the children one evening.

It was now December and Nellie and Connie wanted it to be the best ever for them all as this was to be the last one where they all lived together. Connie had been given a three-bedroomed house in the next road. They had heard on the grapevine that an elderly lady who had lived there for many years had passed away, so both women raced up to the landlord's office where Nellie had previously been going to pay her rent to make some enquiries.

"The landlord was not the friendliest person I have met, kept on about making sure that I could afford the rent. I think as a war widow, which is what I told him, he was concerned that I would not be able to keep up the payments, cheeky sod," complained Connie.

"Thank you, Nellie, you have been an absolute angel to let us live with you for so long, but it is time for you to have your space back again and in reality, the kids need to have more room and privacy as they are getting older. Just imagine they can now have a bedroom each. I can't believe how lucky I have been, getting that house when so many are still having to live two families or more to one house in London."

"Mind you, those few white lies about your parents coming over from Ireland to live with you for a time may have helped," laughed Nellie.

"Well, who knows they may wish to," laughed Connie. "Mind you, it would be wonderful to see them again, it has been years now since I saw them last and writing is not the same. I may once I am settled write and put that suggestion to them though."

Christmas was as wonderful as they had hoped it would be. They had managed to get a small real tree and the trimmings from the market, but it was decided not to put it up indoors too early as the needles looked like they might shed before the big day. Presents were put under the tree on Christmas Eve after the kids had gone to sleep, which like most children is no mean feat the night before Christmas. Eventually, the tired women made their way to bed, after making the mince pies and finishing off the Christmas cake, a carrot and a small glass of milk were left out for Santa and Rudolf, so after they were happy that all was prepared, the lights finally went out.

Christmas morning could not have been more perfect. Outside, everywhere was coated with a dusting of white shimmering heavy frost. Nellie was up first to ensure that it was as magical as possible for the children. She stoked up the fire and it quickly sprang back into life, flames flickered giving the room a wonderful cosy glow. the tree lights were put on, Nellie checked that the presents were all in place and once satisfied that everywhere looked right, she just had time to make herself a cup of tea as she heard the whoops of joy and excitement coming from upstairs.

"Mum, wake up, he's been. Father Christmas has been, he has filled our stockings with things."

Nellie smiled to herself and went back to the kitchen to make a cup of tea ready for Connie. She poured the children a glass of milk each but doubted that it would be drunk in the excitement. The fragrances that filled the house during the day were amazing; never before could they remember it all being so wonderful, especially after all the rationing during the wartime.

Later in the day, when the outside temperature increased and the frost melted away, Billy and Lizzie took their new bikes out and along with the other children in the street, played cycling up and down showing their presents to one another, giving Nellie and Connie a few minutes to put their feet up and have a well-earned cuppa. Roast chicken, potatoes and all the trimmings were served followed by Christmas pudding and cream.

"It was the best Christmas ever and Santa was able to bring us lots of presents and best of all, we both had our new bikes. We love you, Mummy and Aunty Nellie. Night night," said the very tired children as they were tucked back up in bed that night.

"Once again, it is all thanks to our dear departed Mary. She would have loved all of this, because of her the children have had such a grand Christmas with their new bikes and enough food and treats fit to burst. Oh well, maybe she is up there watching over us and sharing the joy. Come on, let's not get maudlin. I shall pour us another sherry and we can pull the sofa nearer to the fire and sit and enjoy a well-earned rest and see out the rest of Christmas day," said Connie as she flopped down onto the sofa.

Both women just sat warming their toes from the embers of the fire, deep in their own thoughts.

Nellie helped Connie move into her new home and between them, made it look nice and homely with a lick of paint here and there, a few nick knacks from Nellie's or the market. They even managed to get their hands on some old curtains that Nellie was able to alter to fit the bedroom windows. It gradually began to feel more homely, the kids were overjoyed and thought that they were dead posh what with having their own rooms where they could spread out.

A routine gradually developed where if Nellie was at home and their mum was still working, they would go to Nellie's for tea after school until Connie returned from work. This pleased Nellie as she still felt very much a part of their young lives and hopefully would always remain so.

Nellie and Connie started to go to play Bingo once a week with some of the women from work. It gave them a night out and extra money in their pockets when they had a win. Once a month, they would get the sitter in to mind the kids while they went off to a dance at a club in Ilford which had a large dance floor and was a vibrant lively place and well-attended. Both women loved to get up and dance and were never short of men to invite them onto the floor. Both, although now older, still retained their good looks and dressed as smartly and with the same pride they had in their younger days. Often men would ask to see them again but generally the girls politely declined.

"I reckon that quite a few of the lads are already married and are out for a bit of fun."

"Well," replied Connie, "so are we."

"No, not the sort of fun that they are looking for. They are most likely looking for a bit on the side. We still have a little work to do with your naivety at times." To this, the girls had a good giggle.

On one occasion when they were on a night out, a young gentleman made advances towards Connie. He appeared to be very smartly dressed and had a less self-assured and more gentlemanly attitude about him. Connie danced a few times with him then returned back to Nellie.

"He seems to be nice, and better than some that are here tonight. You should have stayed on the dance floor longer and get to know him a bit more."

"No, we are here on a girls' night out, so we stick together. Anyway, he does come across as very interesting and polite, so I have agreed to see him again."

Joe, as Nellie soon found out, came from Dublin and during the war was a fighter pilot. Now he was a music teacher and musician who played a guitar, sometimes with a band at clubs. As Nellie got to know him more, she could see for herself the strengthening bond between the two of them.

Connie and Joe saw more and more of one another in the following months, as the relationship blossomed. Nellie was pleased for her friend but was beginning to see less of her, understandably until one day, Connie announced that Joe had asked her to marry him and she had accepted.

"Oh Connie! I am so delighted for you, he certainly appears to be a very good catch and the kids adore him. It is obvious to anyone how much he loves you. When do you plan to marry?"

"I would like to marry in the spring and I would love to have some photos taken out the front under the cherry blossom tree, because you, the house, especially when the blossom is out, are some of the happiest memories in my life."

"That is the loveliest thing to say, Connie. I am so proud, I will make sure that everywhere is clean and swept, so that it looks the best it can be."

"Nellie, the house is always immaculate, but thank you."

As the wedding drew near, Nellie asked, "What are your plans for the future? Will you be moving away from here then?" She was excited for her friend but also anxious in case they had both decided to return to Ireland at some stage in the near future. Although Nellie had made friends in the area and at work, but none compared to the closeness that her and Connie shared.

"No, that was made clear to Joe. I explained that our friendship goes back many years and that the bond between us is strong and so I did not wish to move away, also the kids are very happy and settled here."

"Oh thank goodness, I would have understood if you did move away, but I am so glad that you are staying, I would have missed you all so much."

Nellie made the wedding outfit for Connie and the bridesmaid dress for young Lizzie.

Connie's suit was made in a cream silk fabric which complimented her cream complexion and beautiful red hair which hung in waves around her face. Her green eyes shone with minimal makeup to enhance them.

"Connie, you look absolutely gorgeous. Joe is a very lucky man."

Young Lizzie's dress was also in cream with an emerald sash and bow, giving a nod to their respective homeland.

"I am so happy, let's hope that your Mr Right is just around the corner, Nellie."

"Oh don't worry about me, as you know the love of my life has been and gone, I am perfectly happy with my lot," replied Nellie, although a slight pang of heartache was felt in her chest.

Scotland was the choice of place for their honeymoon, so with a wave of goodbye, Connie and her new husband drove off in Joe's car and headed away for a fortnight and the children returned with Nellie to her house where they would stay until their return.

Nellie loved having the kids stay with her and took a week off work so it made life easier with them going to school.

"We have booked a cottage in Norfolk for us all to have a holiday," said Connie one day. "That includes you, Nellie. The cottage has enough bedrooms for us all and I remember you saying once that you would like to return and see where you once stayed as a land girl."

Preparations were made, bags packed and the car was filled to the brim and off they went heading for Norfolk for a week's holiday.

The cottage was tucked away in a secluded area of Norfolk in a place called Fakenham. There on the grounds was a small lake, not too deep, but enough for a small row boat to go on which the farmer had advised they were perfectly at liberty to use, much to the kids' excitement. Everywhere was functional and spotlessly clean. Everyone had their own bedroom upstairs, the children had a small room each next to Connie and Joe. Nellie's was at the other end of the landing, it was slightly bigger than the others with a chair next to the window. Often she would go and sit next to the window alone to read or just for some privacy. The women shared the cooking while Joe took the kids out in the row boat as they tried to catch fish with small rods that had been found in one of the cupboards. If they had been lucky enough to catch any tiddlers, Joe showed Billy how to gently remove the fish from the hook then return them to the water. Lizzie did not like the idea, so she was content just to be rowed around.

"Can you remember where the farm was, Nellie?" asked Joe one day. "If you wish to go there, we can drop you off and come and pick you up again later."

So off they went in the direction of where Nellie remembered the farm was. With a few wrong turns, she was delighted to find it again.

"It all looks very different than when I was last here!" exclaimed Nellie. Most of the land had been turned over to grow produce. "Now it all looks much greener and smaller than I remember."

"Just see if anyone is there and are happy to invite you in before we drive off and leave you," said Connie.

Nellie, with some trepidation, went to the front door and knocked. After a few moments, she turned and waved to them then disappeared inside the cottage.

"It's young Nellie, isn't it?" said Jenny the farmer's wife after a few moments.

The cottage inside had not changed to much, but it still had a homely feel about it. The tea was quickly made and some homemade scones put on a plate then the two women sat down and chatted away. They talked for ages and fresh tea made while they caught up on events since they last saw one another.

"It was such a shame about your friend in London, but you left so suddenly without leaving a forwarding address," commented Jenny.

"I am so sorry for that but I had to get back to London as quick as I could, I did not think of anything else at the time."

Nellie started to notice how Jenny had aged since she saw her last; mind you, she thought it had to be 15 or more years ago since she left.

"How are your family, have you any grandchildren now?" asked Nellie.

"Our eldest was killed during the war and our younger son sustained injuries at Dunkirk, but at least he is alive, but no, we do not have any grandchildren and I don't suppose we will have. Ah well, that's life. Anyway," asked Jenny, "how are things with you, have you married?"

"Oh, I very nearly forgot!" cried Jenny as she handed Nellie a letter. "It is from that American that you made friends with whilst you were here, he came back a few times to see if you were here then finally he just left this letter for you in the hope that you would return, but that was a good few years ago now."

Nellie's heart took a jolt. Even after all these years, she still thought of him from time to time, wondering how he might be and if he had survived the war. Putting the letter in her handbag, she decided that she would read it in the privacy of her own space.

"How are the other girls that worked here on the farm, have you kept in touch?"

"Samantha married the local farmer that she was seeing when you were here, she now has two children and often calls 'round when she has a minute. The children are great so they have become our adopted grandchildren."

"A bit like me with my friend's children," laughed Nellie.

Connie, Joe and the kids arrived at the agreed time to collect Nellie and after introductions then goodbyes, they returned to the cottage where they were staying.

In her room, Nellie sat for ages just looking at the letter from Michael which was in her hand.

"Oh don't be stupid, you are a grown woman now, not a silly schoolgirl. Just open it," she scolded herself.

My Dearest Nellie

Oh where are you, my love? I returned to my wife after you left, but it was no good, it was not fair to her to stay, when I was so in love with you. How I have missed you, it is torturing me, not knowing where you are or how to get hold of you. I have been back to the farm many times since the war, but no one has seen or heard from you, so I left this letter in the hope that one day you would return and that fate would be kind and give us the chance to be together again. I am now working between London and New York, so I will leave both addresses in the hope that you will make contact again and we can meet.

In the meantime, until we meet again, I give you my love.
Michael.

Nellie read the letter over and over as the tears ran down her cheeks.

"What have I done to deserve life being such a shit to me? So many years have gone by since Michael wrote this letter.

It seems that I am destined never to have happiness in the arms of a man. Why oh why am I being punished?"

Nellie decided that once they had returned home, she would send a letter to both addresses in the hopes of making contact, although by now she was sure that he had given up on her and had met someone else. Once again, Nellie had an unsettled night of mixed dreams.

"Right then, girls, who is ready for a girls' night out?" called out Betty in her loud and booming voice that easily carried over the sounds of the sewing machines as the machines worked away.

"I for one fancy a night in the town, I am fed up sitting night after night with that grumpy old sod of a husband, so I shall put some war paint on and get out there and see what I can pull, knowing my luck it will be a bleedin' muscle."

Everyone laughed, although Betty's language and manner could be coarse at times, she liked to portray a tough exterior but in reality had a heart of gold and would give her last penny if you needed it.

"I am up for that," a chorus of voices replied.

"I reckon we all could do with a bit of a laugh to cheer us up," replied Sheila, another lady who like Betty had a voice that could carry well with a bit of added colour thrown in. "Who knows we might all get lucky. I could do with a bit of slap and tickle, I reckon my old man has forgotten what he has got it for."

Laughter rang out in the factory along with some of the women nodding in agreement.

"How about you, Connie?" asked Nellie. "Fancy a night out with the girls?"

"I am up for it," laughed Connie, "it is always good fun if not boisterous. I am sure that Joe won't mind keeping an eye on the kids, although now they are older they are pretty sensible."

The night out went well and both Nellie and Connie made the effort to look their best and once again, Nellie's skills with the sewing machine came to the fore, with a few changes and embellishments their old dresses looked bang up-to-date and fresh. With a little makeup and their hair done up, they both looked happy and very attractive. Connie with her green eyes, red hair and creamy skin looked as good as she had in their youth, although fast approaching her 40th birthday. As Nellie looked at herself in the mirror, she no longer saw the fresh-faced young woman of her youth but settled for the reflection looking back at her.

"Well, girl, that's as good as it gets."

One her return from work one evening, there was a letter on Nellie's mat. After making herself a cup of tea, she sat in her chair and opened the envelope.

My dearest Nellie

You cannot imagine my surprise and pleasure on receiving your letter. So much time has passed that I had begun to feel that our moment in time would just be a memory. I will be back in London soon and I would love nothing more than for us to meet up. There is so much to catch up on, I could not begin to write it all in a letter. Oh! Nellie, I feel like a young lad again looking forward to Christmas, I am just so excited at the prospect of seeing you again. If you are happy to meet me and I do hope you say yes, then I will confirm my

arrival date and where we can meet. I await your response with the sincere hopes of your agreement. Until then, my love.
Michael xx

Nellie sat and read the letter again, she was now filled with a mixture of excitement and anxiety.

"What should I do, should I meet with him? So much time has passed, will he be the same person I once thought I could love? Will he still like me now that I am older and not the same young free girl I once was?"

"Nellie," advised Connie, "you are bound to be anxious about seeing him again, but you are the same person that he fell in love with. Sure you are now older but so is he and do you not think that he is possibly as concerned as you? But neither of you will know the answers until you meet again. I feel that you should at least meet up because if you don't, you will always regret it. Who knows the flame may be rekindled and a new journey started."

"Connie, am I doing the right thing?"

Nellie's meeting was to be later that day and the nerves were kicking in. She felt excited and sick at the same time. She felt that her stomach was doing somersaults and giving herself a headache. "Honestly, this is ridiculous. I am a grown woman, not a teenager on her first date."

"Nellie, you look absolutely gorgeous. With that little bit of makeup and the outfit that you are wearing shows off your fabulous figure, I would not be surprised if he does not fall in love with you all over again. Just try and relax and enjoy yourself, what have you got to lose?"

Nellie was wearing a dress in cornflower blue which, with her blue eyes and dark brown hair pinned up with soft curls hanging down to frame her face, made her look every bit as lovely as in her youth but with the added bonus of maturity which gave an air of sophistication.

"Oh well, here we go, see you later."

As Connie watched her friend walk away, she felt a tear trickle down her cheek as she thought, *I hope with all my heart the meeting is successful. You deserve some happiness and the chance to love and be loved again.*

"Well, how did it go? Did you meet up on time and did you recognise one another?"

"Ooh we met up without any delay and I recognised him immediately and him me. Obviously he is older, hair is slightly greyer around the sides and has put on some weight, but he is still a handsome man."

"I can sense a but in your voice."

"He has since married again to another American woman, so I asked him why the hell he agreed to meet up with me again. Michael said that he was sure that if he had told me that he was married, then I would not have agreed to meet."

"Too bloody right, it was unfair of him."

"He explained that although he was married, he would dearly love to meet up as just old friends and have a catch up."

"How do you feel about that? So when he is over, you can meet up as friends, do you feel that he wants to have his cake and eat it?" asked Connie.

"I don't know, I must admit that I was very angry when he informed me. I felt foolish and was fully prepared to leave him sitting in the restaurant, but he persuaded me to stay and talk. Eventually, because I did enjoy his company, I decided to stay. He explained that he had given up any hope of ever seeing me again and decided that life must go on and that now we have reunited, he did not want to lose me again and dearly wished for us to be friends. I have to admit that with his dashing smile, blue eyes that held a twinkle, the easy conversation, I made the decision that why cut off my nose, I would be the one to lose out and it's not like I have men falling at my feet to choose from."

"Nellie Brown, whatever would your grandparents have said?"

Both women laughed.

So whenever Michael was in England, Nellie and he would meet and inevitably the relationship moved on to them having an affair. Nellie had accepted that long-term Michael would return to America for good, but she decided that as wrong as it was, she was not going to deny herself the chance to lay in his arms and feel loved and wanted, even if it was only to be a short-term relationship.

Chapter 15

Christmas in the past had been celebrated at Nellie's house. Now with the family having expanded, it was held at Connie and Joe's. Both Billy and Elizabeth had married and now had children of their own. Elizabeth had two girls; Mary (named after Connie's Irish mother) who was now 5 years and a real beauty with her dark hair and blue eyes, not at all after her mother, and Rita, 3 years old who had the colouring of her grandmother with the red hair and green eyes, who was also a spirited child and certainly knew her own mind.

Billy had two children; Danny the boy who was now a very sensible and studious 7 year old, the opposite of his shy sister Kathleen of 4 years, who also had her grandmother's colouring of red hair and green eyes, but unlike her cousin was very quiet and timid, but was always keen to help especially in the kitchen.

Once the children had opened presents in their own homes, they would all go to Granny and Grand Pop's for their Christmas dinner where both Nellie and Connie had prepared a huge spread. It was a tight squeeze to get all the adults and children around the table but they managed and if anything, it added to the fun. Squashed together with the food whizzing back and forth until everyone had everything they wanted on their plates. Conversations would be non-stop as the young cousins forgot their table manners of 'not speaking with food in your mouth'. They all got on so well and there was always plenty to catch up on when they got together.

In the afternoon, they would listen to the Queen's speech on the radio, a tradition she continued on from her father. This was then followed by some traditional Irish songs from both Connie and Joe's homeland. Joe was a very good violinist and singer and often played to entertain the family. Tears would often well up in Connie's eyes as it brought back memories of her parents who had now long gone, but Joe did not linger too long with morose songs but would step it up with jigs and reels where the younger children could dance along. Connie tried to show the girls how to do the traditional Irish dance and they made a very good attempt. When they tried to include young Danny, he would have none of it.

"That's girls' stuff, I'm not dancing."

As had become their tradition at the end of the Christmas festivities, the women both sat with their feet up near the fire and drank their glasses of sherry, reminiscing over their lives and ponder would they have changed anything if they could have. Joe decided to leave the women to relax and enjoy a quiet moment with their sherry, while he went off to the pub for a drink and chat to the locals.

"How fortunes change," commented Connie as she sipped on her second sherry and was mellowing nicely. "To think, our thriving business just started by pure chance, as I suppose many things in life do."

When young Elizabeth was due to marry her young man, Connie asked Nellie if she would make her bride's and bridesmaid dresses, which turned out to be so beautiful that soon orders flooded in, so Nellie converted her front room into her dressmaking area where the business grew. Connie also did her bit, taking the orders and dealing with the financial side of things, so between them they managed a very lucrative business and although they could now afford to move, neither women had any desire to.

As the years rolled on by, Nellie's relationship with Michael had gradually fizzled out as his trips over from America reduced the older he became and the fact that younger men were taking his place.

They remained in contact with Christmas and birthday cards, but even they after a time stopped. Nellie knew that this day would come, but because her life was now so involved with Connie's family and running her now very busy business, she had accepted the inevitable.

"I am sorry that it has ended, Nellie," commented Connie one afternoon while unusually they had a few minutes from working to enjoy a well-earned cup of tea. "I had really hoped that it may have ended better for you."

"It was inevitable, I knew that it would be this way, he would never have come to live in England and I certainly would not go to America. Anyway, he did love his wife even though he had cheated on her for many years, but honestly, I am content with my life I have lived on my own for so long now that I don't feel that I could share it with anyone on a full-time basis. I am too set in my ways. Anyway, I have a family, you and your brood."

One day out of the blue, Connie asked Nellie, "Do you ever feel old at times? I know that I do."

"Give over, Connie, you are still in your prime."

"I don't think so. At 62 years, I am on the downward slope, I just feel so tired at times."

"Well, I am not far behind at 59 years but I still feel as if I have a lot to give. Mind you, I am not surprised that you often feel tired, what with the grandchildren and all the preparations involved at Christmas. Maybe you just need a tonic, go and see your doctor in the new year and get a check-up."

After this, both women just sat quietly, sipping their sherry and lost in their own thoughts.

Seeing in the New Year was celebrated together as it had been since as long as they could remember, again everyone went to Connie and Joe's. Another good reason to have the party at their house was because their house was bigger with three bedrooms, so if the adults had overdone the alcohol intake, which realistically they always did, there was a bed to crash down in. Food was put out on the table, along with crisps and lemonade for the children, and the drinks would flow.

Parties were always such good fun and the grandchildren loved the chance to get together again with their cousins. Music would fill the air with the latest groups along with some old sentimental songs that always took the girls back down memory lane, then at the stroke of midnight, the front door and back door would be opened to let the old year out and the new one in. People would sometimes come out of their houses and call out Happy New Year to one another. Kisses and cuddles would be shared all around and they would join hands to sing 'Auld Lang Syne'.

"It's not as good as it used to be," moaned Connie to her husband.

Years ago, before the docks began to close, there were often ships in the docks that would sound their horns, dustbin lids would be banged by neighbours that had come out into the street, many would form a line and dance and sing to 'The Lambeth Walk' among other popular songs and were joined by more as they danced their way further up the street. Often, the party would then carry on outside for a while or would weave in and out of one another's houses, many probably with more drink in them than they could handle, but everyone was having a great time. Then, from some houses they could hear many other East End songs; 'Knees up Mother Brown', the 'Hokey Cokey'. Neighbours all around joined together just as they did some years before for the Coronation of Queen Elizabeth. Celebrations and street parties were held all over the country.

After seeing in the New Year, the children would be put to bed and the adults would carry on until the early hours.

"Bloody hell!" exclaimed Connie the next day. "When will I learn not to drink so much?"

"Me too," mumbled Nellie, making them a glass of Alka-Saltzer whilst holding her left hand to her head. "Here, drink this, it may help."

"I am going to take Connie on a holiday, somewhere warm I think, as I am concerned about her. She seems to be tired most of the time and is not her usual self," said Joe to Nellie one day. "I have suggested that she not work today if you do not mind, and advised her to rest."

"She mentioned to me some weeks ago that she felt tired and I thought that with all the work that Christmas involves, it may be that, but I did say that she should see the doctor, did she go?"

"Not that I am aware of, or if she did, she has not said anything. I have booked a week in Spain, it is supposed to be nice and warm there even this early in the year, then when we return, I will insist that she sees the doctor."

"Well," asked Nellie, "what did the doctor say?"

Nellie noted that even though Connie had spent a week relaxing in the sun, she did not look much better. If anything, she still looked tired and drawn. Connie tried hard to hide how she was really feeling by talking about their holiday and how much they had enjoyed it. Nellie had known Connie for far too long to be fooled by her cheerfulness.

"He has referred me to a specialist at the hospital, I have an appointment for next week."

"I am sure that they will get to the bottom of it and get you sorted out," Nellie said with a smile, but not convincing herself.

"Oh, my God, Nellie," said Connie as she sat in the armchair in her sitting room. Joe was standing next to her and the look on his face did not help to reassure Nellie.

"The consultant feels that I may have A form of Leukemia he wants to carry out more tests before he will confirm his suspicions and has tried to offer some hope by explaining that this illness has various types, so once he knows which one I have, he can treat me accordingly. It certainly explains why I have been experiencing my symptoms."

"Well, let's try to be positive. Once they know what they are dealing with, they can commence the right treatment for you and get you right again," said Nellie.

Connie was not so lucky. Her symptoms were more advanced than anticipated.

Various treatments were tried over the months but nothing appeared to be working. Eventually, they all had to accept the fact that it was time to enjoy their life and make the most of it for as long as they were able, and so they did.

Connie wished to be in her own home as the time drew near with her family around her. The room was to be filled with music. Joe had once given a record to Connie on one of her birthdays and it was a favourite of hers; it was lively Irish jigs and reels along with soft ballads. Connie smiled as she heard the music playing.

Previously at many a party, the Irish music had been proudly played to the enjoyment of the neighbours.

"That music is sure to get your feet tapping and make you get up for a dance," the neighbours would say.

Life would never be the same again after the loss of Connie. Nellie and she had been close friends for so many years and had been through so much together. She tried hard to be strong and support Joe and the rest of the family, but she desperately struggled to come to terms with her own grief. Nellie had never felt so utterly alone.

Life held no interest any more for Nellie. She no longer had the appetite for dress making and stopped taking orders. Also she was finding that in this new modern world, fashion items could be purchased and mass-produced so much cheaper now. The high street shopping also was so different for the younger generation than anything she had previously experienced.

"Nellie girl, it is time to put away your needles and pins and accept the fact that you are past it."

Often Nellie would forget to eat anything and would often just sit looking out of the window, wondering why everyone she ever loved and cared for had gone from her life leaving her feeling so very lonely. If she did venture out for any bits of shopping, she found herself to be grumpy and did not want to get into conversation with anyone. Even the street life that she loved and remembered was totally changed. Many families now had cars parked outside their houses, where once the women would be outside cleaning their windows and scrubbing the pathways to their front doors seemed to be a thing of the past. Front doors would at one time been left open and the women would call out to the kids playing in the street to nip and get a bit of shopping for them. Nowadays, doors would be closed if you dared to complain to the kids for playing ball up against the wall more often than not, they gave some back chat.

Nellie felt a stranger in the street where she had spent all her married life. Foreign people had come into the country to live and work, new towns were springing up as more houses and areas to live had to be built. Nellie tried hard to come to terms with all of the changes and had she still had Connie, she probably would have and the pair of them would have a good laugh about it all, but since the loss of her closest friend, she struggled to carry on. Joe would sometimes take her out in the car and often take her for dinner at either Billy's or Lizzie's house, but no matter how hard she tried, she could not shake off this feeling of utter loneliness and melancholy.

Then one day, a good while after the loss of Connie, Billy and his family arrived to take Nellie on a holiday to Cornwall. They did not give Nellie any warning of their plans as they knew that she would put up objections. Billy had a job in London and with a good salary, he was able to buy a car big enough to take his wife, children and Nellie. Nellie attempted to object but to no avail, so a bag of clothes were hurriedly put together along with toiletries and before Nellie could draw breath, they headed off on their long journey to Cornwall.

It had been many years since Nellie had felt sand under her feet and heard the waves gently rolling in, the smell of the salt in the air brought back many memories, but strangely enough, instead of making her feel sad, she actually enjoyed reliving some of the fun she had experienced in the past and at last felt she was coming out from the dark place that she had been trapped in for so long. Returning back in the evening to where they were staying and eating fish and chips from the paper wrappings had never tasted so good.

Nellie could not thank them all enough for taking her away on holiday as it had the desired effect that Billy had hoped for and that Nellie really appreciated.

From that time on, Nellie again felt that she was back in the ever-changing society.

"I hope that you do not mind my cheek, Nellie, but I desperately need to go into London for an appointment in a week's time and I really don't want to take my baby. I know that I am asking a lot and that we are almost strangers, but I have seen you many times and you seem to be such a lovely kind lady when I watch you play with your grandchildren, so would it be possible for you to look after Julia for me, please? I will pay, of course. My name's Maggie, by the way."

Nellie had seen Maggie pushing the pram down the street many times and was impressed by the way she always had a smile for the people that she met, was very smart looking and how the pram would gleam in the sunshine.

Nellie invited the young woman in and offered her a cup of tea. While the baby remained asleep, the young woman chatted away to Nellie and informed her that her husband's name was John. He worked in the local docks and they had only recently moved into the street.

Maggie and Nellie instantly hit it off, they chatted for quite some time getting to know one another. Nellie explained about the children and gave a brief history of Connie and that they were her grandchildren. Nellie suggested that Maggie return another day when Julia was awake so that they could meet one another and ensure that the baby was happy with Nellie, which Maggie did and before she attended her appointment, the two women had become good friends.

So now in her early 60s, Nellie had a little smile to herself as she thought how time was constantly on the move and that now she was acting as the Granny she lost so many years before and how she was now taking young Maggie under her wing.

Chapter 16

Nellie was now nearing her 80th birthday and celebrations were being organised by Billy and Elizabeth along with their families, who were now themselves adults.

Nellie had over the years become a great friend and help to her near neighbour Maggie, who looked upon Nellie as a second mother and certainly did more to help than her own mother. Looking after Julia had been a joy for Nellie, allowing Maggie to get herself a small part-time job at that time. Julia, who was now a grown woman, continued to call Nellie Granny Brown, which had been bestowed on Nellie from the moment the child was able to talk. It had taken Nellie some time to get over the loss of her very dear friend and many times when something interesting happened, Nellie for a moment would want to relay it to Connie, then she had to remind herself that that time was gone.

Nellie felt old and that she had outlived her time. So many changes had occurred; her front room that had been her and Connie's sewing room was now turned back with furniture and long gone was the sewing machine and fabrics that once earned her some money along with her enjoyment. Clothes were now so much cheaper in the retail stores and with such a large selection for all ages and sizes to choose from, it was so easy to go in and just pick something ready-made off the hanger to wear.

"Wow, what we would have given in our youth to have such a choice instead of the utility wear we had, although in my day, we had the attention of an assistant who would help to choose an outfit and advise if something suited or not." Nellie occasionally would go shopping along with Elizabeth and her daughters, but she was never over keen as she found once you stepped over the threshold, it could be a little intimidating. Music would be playing and often very busy, people would be milling around and pulling out rows and rows of clothes to inspect them with a freedom to just wander, although she did enjoy and was often amazed at what the youngsters were buying.

My granny would be mortified if I had worn something like that, she laughed. Nellie thoroughly enjoyed going for lunch with the girls after the shopping trips and they would often sit and gossip for ages, also she was so grateful to them all for continuing to include her in their lives, she admitted that although she loved her house and would only leave it in her box, she really missed having company.

Food shopping was more enjoyable for Nellie; she loved the variety that was available on the shelves, even impressed by the foreign foods on display, although she never ventured to try any.

"I suppose if I had any complaint about the modern supermarkets, it is the lack of personal service. Everything slides along the conveyor belt and then you pay. If I did not shop with you, Elizabeth, I would not be quick enough to put the shopping into my bag before someone tutted at me."

"Since when have you been afraid to give them an answer, Gran, they would soon get the sharpness of your tongue."

"I thought that I was mellowing nicely," laughed Nellie.

Youngsters seemed to have more money at their disposable, there was so much more for them to do, but again Nellie felt that although there had been many advancements in the world, so had a lot been lost. Everything seemed to move fast and the days where neighbours would leave their front doors open were gone. The majority of women now worked and had careers of their own, so the street where Nellie lived where once front doors were left open during most of the day were now tight shut resulting in the fact she may not see anyone from one end of the day to the other, especially in the winter. There did not seem to be the local community spirit that was once there. Once upon a time, people would stand and chat to the rent man calling or even the milkman when he came to collect his money, the rag and bone man that would come down the streets calling out for any old rags.

Time marched on and Nellie gradually started to go out less and less with the girls. She still enjoyed their company but the shopping trips she gradually found were becoming less manageable, (not that she would admit that to the girls).

"I don't know as I care too much for this modern way, I often feel more lonely now than I ever did before."

Oh, Nellie knew that she was better off than many, at least she had visitors once in a while and young Maggie would get her any bits of shopping if she was unable to get out herself, which in truth, Nellie was not so keen to venture out too far on her own. Unknown to others, she had had the odd fall when indoors and was frightened that she may do the same outside.

She tried desperately to hide any bruises that she had sustained from any of her family's sharp eyes.

"Oh Nellie," she grumbled to herself one day when it was drizzling, "I can't even get out into my garden today, sod it. Come on gel, stop feeling sorry for yourself and find something to keep busy."

With this, she went and found under her bed a large box which after blowing off the dust, she carried downstairs into her now front room, which was once the sewing room. Here she could look out of the window onto the street and more importantly, look at her much-loved and admired cherry blossom tree.

Sitting in her favourite chair which was many years old as the lack of springs could testify, she proceeded to open the box.

"Jesus, I have not opened this in years."

It was a container that over the years Nellie had thrown all her little keepsakes in. It had so much stuff inside it that the lid would only just about close and she had been promising herself that one day, she would tidy it all up, but it then always got pushed back under the bed for another day. Nellie decided the best way was to tip everything out onto the floor and pick up a piece at a time, examine it, then put into a wanted or not wanted pile, then the wanted would be returned in the box.

"Mind you, gel," she mumbled to herself, "by hoarding all these mementos when I pop my clogs, it is just more junk for someone else to clear up, as it will mean nothing to them."

Nellie proceeded to tip everything out of the box, which smelt musty as there had been many years of keepsakes thrown in. "Bloody hell, now I can see why I kept on putting it off. There are mountains of the stuff, I think I need a cuppa to help me along, I will surely get dry in the time this lot will take me."

Nellie should have also got herself a box of hankies at the same time as she tripped down memory lane.

Photos of her nan and granddad standing at the front gate waving her off to work. Photos of her Tommy in the early days of their courtship along with a couple of letters Tommy had sent when he had first joined up with the navy. The train tickets to Southend where they spent their honeymoon, the telegram from the war office informing her of the loss of Tommy.

A simple red button that at some stage had come off her uniform when she was a Nippy working in London where she first became friends with Connie. Dance tickets that the girls had attended during the war time. Somehow she had an old rent book that the girls were first given when they moved in with Mary in Bethnal Green, which once a firm friendship had been established was dispensed with.

Wiping some tears from her eyes and cheeks and taking a few mouthfuls of her tea, Nellie then continued on.

The train ticket to Norwich where she worked as a Land girl and lived on a farm with two other girls. The newspaper cutting of the disaster at Bethnal Green which took the life of her beloved Mary. Bernie's letter, the man that she had rescued from the London bombings and was left blind. He had written to Nellie a few years earlier to inform her that he had married a lady that worked in his father-in-law's company, who was more than happy to give his blessing to the marriage and encouraged them to continue working for him.

Many more little things that over the years held special memories were secreted in the box, often something would tug on her heart strings as she remembered the time and event associated with the item,

"Oh!" she exclaimed out loud. "Some of these memories feel like they happened only yesterday, not years ago."

These are the golden threads that have weaved into the tapestry of my life, thought Nellie.

Lastly, another small box was found right at the bottom of the large box. In fact, she could easily have missed it. As Nellie gently opened it, there inside was a dried rose which once would have been red, along with one of Connie's much-loved flowers. It was a dry piece of shamrock from her homeland. These were the flowers Nellie had kept from the funeral of her beloved friend many years before. Gently as she lifted the very fragile flowers to her lips, tears began to sting her eyes and gradually rolled down her cheeks, then unbidden more tears escaped until she was no longer in control.

Nellie began to cry like she had not done for many years, all of her past flooded back in.

"Where has the time gone and all so quickly? My family and friends all moved on, so much happiness and heartache, but in its own way, it has been a very full life." Tears continued to flow as Nellie picked up the snippets of memories and revisited them in her mind.

The following day, Nellie woke up feeling more positive about her future. Feeling now she had visited the past she was able to pack them away safely in her heart and allow them to rest whilst she would embrace whatever her future may bring.

In the days and weeks after, Nellie began to sort out various pieces of jewellery, furniture ornaments and so on that people had shown a particular fondness for and to write a will as to her wishes of who was to have what.

Small token items she knew that her neighbour Maggie had shown interest in, one of them being just an old salt pot that had belonged to Nellie's gran being one of them, most things were of no monetary value just mementoes which had been obtained during her life.

Nellie's house was to be sold along with the furniture and the proceeds to be divided equally between Billy and Elizabeth.

"I suppose that I have lived for so bleedin' long, most of what I have are now classed as antiques like me," smiled Nellie to herself.

Once Nellie was satisfied that many of her things of any good had been entered into her will, she then set about cleaning her house from top to bottom. The house was always kept immaculately clean and tidy, just as her grandmother's had been.

"What are you doing Nellie?" asked Maggie one day when she called in as she saw Nellie cleaning her windows.

"I just fancied doing a bit of spring cleaning and freshening the place up," replied Nellie.

"You know that I will do that for you, you should not be reaching up so far, you could hurt yourself."

"I may be dead in my box tomorrow, so while I can, I will," was the quick reply.

So she continued sprucing up the house as she had always done when able and no one was going to tell her to stop.

Once she was happy that the house was clean to her standard and everywhere smelt fresh and clean, she allowed herself a rest. The following day, she felt very tired, so unusually for her she did not get up at her usual time but allowed herself a lie in until 8 am. After her usual routine of washing and dressing, she went downstairs for breakfast.

Later that morning, she got a few belongings together in a small case and carried them back downstairs, which even Nellie had to admit was becoming a bit of a struggle.

"Well gel, today is the day!" Then after making a cup of tea, she returned to her armchair.

"Good morning, Aunt Nellie," a familiar voice woke her from a deep sleep.

As she stirred slowly from her dreams, there in front of her was Billy and his wife Carol.

"I see you have already put a few things in a case, have you got your party dress in there, ready to celebrate your birthday?" asked Billy. "We will return later and pick up some more bits and pieces for you, but for now if you have all you need, are you ready to go?"

"Just give me a few more minutes to say goodbye?" asked Nellie.

"Take as long as you like, I shall just go and put your things in the boot of the car."

Nellie walked from room to room, kissing her hands then touching the walls. "Thank you, house, for giving me so many memories over the last 60 years. I came here with Tommy as a young bride of 22 years and now leaving you as an old lady of 80 years and starting a new millennium. I hope that your new family will love you and look after you as I have tried to do."

With that, Nellie walked to the front door and left without looking back. Outside the house, she was surprised to see so many of her neighbours waiting to wave her off. Bouquets of flowers were given along with many cards and best wishes. Some of the children had balloons which they gave to her.

"What the hell is going on here? I don't know half of these people," she said to Maggie.

"But they know you, Nellie; you are the longest person to have lived in this street and over many years, you have helped these people and looked after their children, so you will be missed very much. This is our way of saying thank you and wishing you all the best for the future. We also wish you a very happy birthday. Enjoy your celebrations, you deserve it."

With this, Maggie and Julia handed over what was to become a most treasured gift. A framed photograph of her house with the cherry blossom tree in full bloom.

Nellie tried desperately to fight back the tears as she quietly said "Thank you" to all her well-wishers as she got into the car.

As Billy left the street for the last time, she would not turn around as she was afraid that she might change her mind, but wondered how her life would be, living out her days near the coast that she so loved in the annex that Billy had built, adjoining his house down in Kent.

The End